EXPOSED

Also by Alison Tyler

Best Bondage Erotica
Best Bondage Erotica 2
The Happy Birthday Book of Erotica
Heat Wave: Sizzling Sex Stories
Luscious: Stories of Anal Eroticism
The Merry XXXmas Book of Erotica
Red Hot Erotica
Slave to Love: Sexy Tales of Erotic Restraint
Three-Way: Erotic Stories

EXPOSED
The Erotic Fiction of Alison Tyler

FOREWORD BY FELICE NEWMAN

Published in the United States by Cleis Press Inc.,
P.O. Box 14697, San Francisco, California 94114.

Printed in the United States.
Cover design: Scott Idleman
Cover photograph: Victoria Perelet
Text design: Frank Wiedemann
Cleis Press logo art: Juana Alicia
First Edition.
10 9 8 7 6 5 4 3 2 1

"The Last Deduction" was published in Great Britain in 2001 and 2004 in the collection *Wicked Words 5* by Black Lace, Thames Wharf Studios, Rainville Road W69HA.

For SAM

I often think that a slightly exposed shoulder emerging from a long satin nightgown packed more sex than two naked bodies in bed.

—BETTE DAVIS

ACKNOWLEDGMENTS

To Judy, who took the first story, and to VK, who wouldn't take the second.

To Richard, who was sorry when I spilled the water, and to Tristan, who told me not to worry about it.

To Thomas for insisting that Violet was real.

To Violet, who was.

To Barbara, who always gives me a chance and a decent deadline.

To Adam, who wishes I'd kept my orchid pumps.

To Felice Newman and Frédérique Delacoste, who had faith.

To my first and to my last.

And to Mr. NN, who bought me that drink.

Contents

FOREWORD

I wish the characters in Alison Tyler's stories lived on my street. I want to live next door to the girl in "Heat" who seduces her boss's husband. She can squeeze the lime in my Evian any time.

The girl who lulls herself to sleep fantasizing about sex with strangers can take up residence at my neighborhood cafe—"I think about sucking him hard, sucking to the very root of his cock, deep-throating him to show how much I want him, how much I want to give him pleasure with my mouth. And I do." ("Yeah")

I want the girl with the knife fetish ("Blades"). And the one who steals panties from the laundry basket, inhaling their fragrance night after night ("Other People's Panties"). And the woman with the scorched earth policy in "Four on the Floor": She and her husband seduce other couples. No apologies. Meet 'em, greet 'em, fuck 'em. And they aren't very nice about it. Who wants nice when we're talking serious tangled-up-on-the-floor sex?

The characters in these stories know that bad girls *do* have all the fun. Yet they're not too bad to notice they're on the precipice of that downward slide. Truth is, Alison's characters are caught in that delicious moment of falling, their panties sticky and clinging, their heat and wetness warning *danger*.

As her editor, I am the paid voyeur of Alison's desire for exposure. I have the front row seat, and I reap the benefits. Her fantasies satisfy mine. (After all, it doesn't take a rocket scientist to figure out that someone who reads porn for a living might be a bit of a voyeur.)

More importantly, Alison's willingness to expose her own fantasies gives others permission to enjoy theirs. You might say that's our mission at Cleis Press—to make it possible for everyone to create authentic and fulfilling sex lives and gender identities. We've done this through a quarter century of publishing the best books on sexuality and gender politics, the best sex guides, and the best erotic fiction available. If our culture has become as sexually permissive as right-wingers say it is (don't you wish?), then I hope we have contributed a hefty share of that permission.

Alison Tyler is one of my favorite erotica authors. Simply put, she makes me hot. Her stories ring true. They are accessible, well crafted, and full of surprises. Each one is as fresh as the Ivory soap-scrubbed girls whose randy enthusiasm fuels their plots. And did I mention they're hot?

Alison is also prolifically loyal to her fetishes: It can't come as a shock that someone who has written as numerous erotic stories and novels as she has might crave exposure as much as her most exhibitionistic protagonists. She's also edited the work of many other excellent erotica writers in her anthologies. You might say that Alison Tyler is among the great curators of smut.

Of course I don't live on a street peopled by Alison Tyler

characters. I have my own neighbors—and my own fantasies. No doubt, you have your own fantasies populated by hot women and men in single-minded pursuit of sex. Perhaps Alison has already contributed a few. Your dirty mind will be so much richer (and dirtier) for having experienced Alison's. Read on.

Felice Newman
San Francisco
April 2006

INTRODUCTION

I used to be twenty-two and into drama. I used to crave that feeling in the base of my stomach that meant things weren't going right. The up-all-night, guilt-shivers made me weak with what I believed was sexual intensity. I looked at people I knew I shouldn't. I yearned for the types of touches that would send me reeling with desire. That's how I ended up with tall, redhaired Anthony, in the back of a fancy gourmet market, letting him feel me up and kiss me while customers averted their eyes. How I ended up with the slim Brit named Adrian, outside against the Crayola-red bricks, my hand on the crotch of his worn jeans, my breathing hard and fast. How I ended up with the beautiful Eden, at the movie theater, kissing each other so madly that we never saw a single frame of the film....

And all while I was engaged to be married.

Then suddenly I was twenty-three, and twenty-four, and twenty-five, and the drama part started to get old. You can only go through so many breakups, standing outside on a balcony and screaming until hoarse, before you realize that although you might live in Hollywood, you don't live in a Hollywood movie. And although you might dress like a starlet, people aren't paying to watch you act.

That doesn't mean I was cured of my desires. It only means that I learned to channel my need for excitement, to find my thrills in a different way. One bleak afternoon, as I sat outside drinking a shot in the dark at King's Road Cafe, I realized that I didn't need the drama of a breakup to make me feel alive. What I truly craved was the feeling of being exposed.

Exposed for what I wanted.

Exposed for who I really am.

Luckily, you can get that need filled even when you're in a relationship. If you know how to play your cards right, you can get that need filled whenever you want it. Exposure is something you can revel in all by yourself. Exposure is the other half of voyeurism. And exposure is something I do daily in my work.

I've danced around the concept with my writing for years, playing peekaboo with truth and fiction. I reveal a little too much, and then duck back undercover, hiding out in safety until the need consumes me yet again. I tell secrets, but change the names. I make up locations, but reveal my emotions. I wrap my truth up in lies, spreading my stories thin, so thin that you can see the real me if you look closely enough. If you take the time to really see.

This collection features erotica I wrote when I was first starting out ("Untouched") and brand-new stories ("Well Trained"). I've pulled together several of my all-time favorites ("Wanna Buy a Bike?" and "The Lindy Shark"), and positioned them with the stories I receive the most mail about ("Girls of Summer" and "Ten Minutes in the Eighties"). Rereading some of these pieces took me back in time ("Heat") and to long-ago vacations ("View from Paris" and "Lost in the Translation").

What I realized as I read through my files during the difficult selection process was that even after more than four hundred stories, fifteen novels, and twenty anthologies, I am still playing coy, glancing out from under my long dark lashes—looking, looking away, looking back. I am a flirt. I readily admit to it. Because there is that tempting quality in all flirts. We want someone to grab us, to hold us under a bright light, to see us for who we really are.

To expose us.

That's all I want. It's all I've ever needed.

Alison Tyler
San Francisco
March 2006

GIRLS OF SUMMER

B oys of Summer" came out right when I finished high school. I went to the beach with my friends every day, all day long, and it seemed as if that's the only song the deejays played. I'm exaggerating, of course, but that's all I remember. That and the scent of tropical suntan oil. No sunblock for us. No SPF 45, or 62, or 1006, or whatever the kids are using these days. We wanted oil, the lowest protection available, and we rotated, as if on spits, to get the most even tan.

My girlfriends kept their eyes open under their ever-so-cool Wayfarers, searching the Santa Cruz beach for cute surfers and college boys. I kept my eyes shut, picturing my recent ex, a man, not a boy, who had not actually broken my heart, but had somehow managed to leave town with that most vital organ in his possession. Since he'd disappeared, I didn't feel anything. Not happy. Not sad or angry or confused. I cruised on empty—not interested in anything but a tan.

Every so often, one of my pals would say, "Oh, Carla, open your eyes. Look at *him*," as some blond Adonis made his way toward us. I'd peek from beneath half-closed lids, toss out a number on a scale of one to ten, then shut my eyes again. We spent all day at the beach, because we didn't have anywhere else to go. In the fall, we'd all be scattered at universities around the country. Until then, we lived at home, occasionally working odd in-between sorts of jobs, like hostess at Chevy's or checkout girl at Whole Foods. We had bonfire nights and went to midnight movies. But mostly we baked until bronze beneath the summer sun. The chicklets in my group all yearned for the heat of a summer romance, while I let the sound of the waves take me back three months to the last time I'd seen my man.

You're not supposed to *have* a man when you're in high school. You're supposed to have nerves about SATs, and tantrums about your curfew, and giggling fits with your girlfriends when some dork feels you up at prom. But I escaped that nonsense by losing my heart to a man, a twenty-seven-year-old rebel who looked like James Dean, dealt cocaine to the executive assholes in Silicon Valley, and picked me up after study hall on his stolen Harley-Davidson.

In my defense, I didn't know about the coke or the fact that his bike was stolen until long after he disappeared. I didn't know that he'd spent time in jail, or that he had a tattoo of the Zig-Zag man on his forearm beneath a bandage he always wore in my presence. I didn't even know who the Zig-Zag man was. All I knew was that at the sweet fresh age of eighteen, I'd learned that nothing about high school really mattered, that none of the teenage problems my friends worried over had any significance to the real world. My boyfriend, the man who fucked me in a twenty-dollar motel room in East Palo Alto, positioning me on top of him with my thighs spread wide, insisting that I look into his deep blue eyes as he made me come—*that* man, was gone. And the phone number he'd given me now reached a recorded voice stating the line had been disconnected. And when I finally tracked down his best friend by hanging out in front of the bar in Menlo Park the two frequented, he told me the real deal about my ex and then gave me the less-than-brilliant advice no one with a broken heart has ever been able to follow:

"Do yourself a favor, kid," he said. "Forget he even existed."

Apply more oil. Turn and roll.

Here I was, with all my pretty credentials, and none of them mattered at all. Nothing mattered except my tan.

Up until I met Mark, I was one of the smart girls, destined for UCLA, a National Merit finalist with four years of Latin, a weekly column in the student newspaper, and a truckload of extracurricular bullshit on my high school "résumé." Now that he was gone, I didn't care. Yeah, I'd go off to school in September, for want of anything better to do, but I didn't care. Yeah, that blond Hercules leaving the crashing California surf was definitely a 9.9 on the Richter scale, but I didn't care.

"Boys of Summer" played endlessly, and I oiled up, and rolled over, and imagined Mark and me on the day I'd taken my spring finals. He picked me up outside the auditorium and kissed me hard, in front of everyone, before driving me off to his tiny apartment on the Atherton/Redwood City border. It caused a stir among my posse, but all that mattered was the rumble of the Harley between my legs, and the way Mark looked at me when he led me up the stairs to his second-floor apartment.

He looked at me as if I were a woman, not some air-brained teen that nobody wanted to take seriously. He fucked all the test questions right out of my head, bent me over his bed and did me doggie-style. And let me tell you, high school boys don't know what doggie-style is. You need a man, a man with a will, a man whose hand comes down on your naked ass and makes you scream while he fucks you. At least, that's what *I* needed.

More oil, now. Scent of pineapples surrounding me.

I never thought about the future when the two of us were together. Although I didn't know for sure what he did when he wasn't with me, I had a feeling he was no Boy Scout. Yeah, I was naive. But I wasn't an idiot. (Couldn't be an idiot. I was a National Merit finalist after all, right?) I knew "importing and exporting" had to be code words for something underhanded. I knew that he wasn't dealing in handwoven baskets from some third-world country. So I lived for the times that we were together. I lived to go down on my knees in front of him and un-button his fly with my teeth the way any good little slut should. I lived to feel his cock slide between my gently parted lips. I lived to swallow him to the hilt, to work him until his cum filled my mouth and I was breathless with the scent of him.

And then he was gone. And it was summer.

"Look at him, Carla. Look at him!"

Before he left, Mark made love to me in my bedroom, while my parents were holding a dinner party just down the hall. He taught me how to go down on him in our den, behind a door with no lock, while we were supposed to be innocently watching a horror video. ("They're coming to get you, Barbara! There's one now...") He grabbed my hair whenever he kissed me, wound his firm fist in my long tresses, and held me in place for the brutality of his kisses.

Brutal. That's what his kisses were. Believe me. I can still close my eyes and taste them. I always felt bruised when we parted. That was okay. I wanted bruised. I wanted the heat of his body pressed to mine. I wanted that rock-hard cock of his, sheathed only in his faded Levi's, slamming against my body when we made out on the couch. He was dangerous, and I needed danger. You don't get danger in the darkened gymnasium of a high school dance. Not even if the boys have been drinking—and they've *always* been drinking. Not even if your lab partner, the cute dark-haired nimrod who cribs your answers during chem finals, tries to get you to go behind the bleachers with him. No, you get danger when you cut class to meet your man, and he dangles a pair of sterling silver handcuffs in front of your eyes, and says, "Baby, you've been a bad girl. We've got to deal with that fact today." And your heart stops, and you look down, and you know that you're going to have to wear long-sleeved shirts for at least a week, even though it's hot as hell out. You get danger when your man lifts your skirt in public and spanks your ass hard for giving him a sassy answer. "Don't talk back, girl, or Daddy'll have to spank you."

High school boys don't have cuffs.

High school boys haven't ever heard of spanking.

High school boys would never, ever have you call them "Daddy."

"Come on, Carla. He's sublime. Open your eyes!"

I'd already opened them. I'd already seen what a man could do.

So I baked all summer long. Oiled up with my long black hair loose, the sand so hot beneath the blanket. I sipped cool drinks of vodka-spiked lemonade, and occasionally indulged in views of handsome boys spearing the surf with their boards. And I thought of Mark somewhere far away. In jail? Maybe. Dead? Maybe. Give me a multiple choice—I knew how to answer that sort of question. Real life? That was a whole different story.

School would change me. I knew that. If Mark could make high school disappear, then college could erase him.

The radio played on and on for the girls of summer.

But I was lost in a future fall.

WELL TRAINED

My men have always been vice afflicted. Sleek to the bone with insomniacs' purple smudges under their eyes. You know the type. Pool hall junkies. Bartending actors. Razor sharp, they've owed their delectably hard bodies to the debauchery of espresso and cigarette breakfasts at noon, not an unnatural devotion to treadmills before dawn.

Until Granger.

When I caught sight of him at a birthday party for a friend, I noted his shaved head and his lean, foxy face and thought, *Just my type.* I didn't know that the drink in his hand was imported water, not imported vodka. Didn't know that his chiseled good looks came from hours of training sloths with no willpower rather than from forgoing three square meals in favor of a double shot of Johnny Walker and a Marlboro Red. I didn't need someone to critique my lifestyle, to throw out my beloved Froot Loops in favor of bland rabbit food, to try and pinch an

inch on my waist, or anywhere else. My years of bad habits have
made me who I am—and I will change for no man. Marlena
claims this is why I'm single. In general, unless I'm feeling particularly lonely, I ignore her.

"Handsome, isn't he?" Marlena asked. She'd caught me
flirting.

"And then some," I agreed.

"So sign up."

"There's a waiting list to fuck him?" I could feel the smile
meet my eyes.

"No, to train with him," she explained to my horror. "His
name is Granger and he owns Rush, the gym on Fourth Street."
I'd been hoodwinked. He didn't look like a trainer—not my
idea of one, anyway. Sure, he had a tight body in his simple
black cashmere sweater and well-cut gray slacks, but he didn't
appear overly muscle-bound. There were no rippling biceps, no
Mr. America inverted-triangle-shaped physique, top-heavy upper body tapering to a tiny, girlish waist. I couldn't imagine him
gleaming bronze beneath bright white lights, striking pose after
pose for an audience of hooting female fans.

As I watched, he casually stroked the lower back of the redhaired woman at his side. She was wearing a formfitting emerald
dress with an oval cutout that dipped dangerously low in the
rear. I could see her structured arms, her superior posture, the
way she seemed to radiate an inner strength.

Was this luminous woman a girlfriend, a client, or both?

I stared, transfixed, as his fingers lingered again at the lowest
point of the dress, more forcefully this time. At his touch, she
turned automatically to face him, as if well trained. An image
flickered in my mind—an image of him in worn black leather
and me at his side, not in a dress, but stripped totally bare,
not standing as his equal, but on my knees on the floor at his

feet—then immediately that vision was gone.

"I'm no gym rat," I reminded Marlena, losing interest. "I don't do trainers." The thought of discussing whey-shakes and tight glutes made me nauseous.

"Break your rules," she advised. "And try this one."

I shook my head, my shiny black bob swinging gently over my cheeks. Sure I live in California, but I'm not nutty *or* crunchy. And although I am acquainted with people who jog, I've never been a fan of the pink-cheeked glow of health that comes from excessive physical activity. When I see studs pumping iron out at Muscle Beach, I turn my head away from their glistening, sweat-drenched figures—not in heart-pounding lust, but in embarrassment. They look like nothing more than caged animals behind the cool silver wrought-iron fence, steroid-enhanced freaks putting on a show for the masses.

"He's a total sadist, you know," she added gleefully, her eyes still focused on Granger's handsome visage. I stared at her, incredulous. She'd said my buzzword.

"What do you mean?" I tried to hide the excitement in my voice.

"There's no other possible excuse," she continued, now turning to face me. "He loves punishing women. Pushing them to their very limits, demolishing every last bit of their sense of self before building them up from scratch again." And now she laughed, drunkenly, and tossed her blonde shoulder-length curls in her look-at-me way that tends to get her what—and *who*—she wants.

Did she know? Could she guess?

When I stared harder at her, I realized that she had no idea what her whispered giggly confession had done to me. I looked back at Granger, deeply curious.

I go for hoodlums and dark horses, men who have the

strength to take me beyond my boundaries. I like after-hours clubs, black velvet, dark smoky places. After being in charge all day long, I like to give myself over to someone else. To someone who knows, who understands the urges that live within me. Brightly lit rooms equipped with shiny gym equipment and floor-to-ceiling mirrored walls do nothing for my libido.

But *sadist*—she'd called him that. And as I looked over at him again, I felt his cold blue eyes returning the appraisal. I considered what he was seeing. My body is slender and toned, but not from hours climbing walls or walking moveable, gray, rubberized tracks to nowhere. I simply can't be bothered with the guilt that always accompanies a gym membership, and the inevitable failure to use it. My lifestyle is workout enough, slamming myself up against deadline after deadline. When the health freaks all did Tae Bo, I had Thai food. When the new rage was yoga performed in a hellishly hot room, I took a relaxing sauna. I'll admit to a single run-in with a gym rat, way back in high school, a man who could bench-press three of me if he'd wanted to. A man who couldn't comfortably bend his arms all the way because the bulges of muscles interfered. It was amusing to watch him try to eat soup, the bicep rippling as he attempted to bring spoon to mouth. It was amusing being bench-pressed, quite honestly, but when that turned out to be his one and only party trick, I lost interest...and found interest in the guys who hung out *behind* the gym—the stoners and slackers and goth writers who wore all black. The motorcycle mavericks who favored faded denim and beaten-in leather. I developed a taste for beer and smoke on the lips of my lovers. What would I possibly do with someone who liked neon-green wheatgrass juice and freshly blanched almond paste?

Or rather, what would *he* do with someone like me?

Yet I found myself staring, calculating, considering. It had been a good long while since my last relationship. And who was saying anything here about a relationship at all? Fucking a trainer was different from dating one, right? I'm strong willed. I could keep my sense of self intact. I wouldn't be like the girl at his side, the one who moved her body at the silent instruction of his fingertips. The one who seemed invisibly connected to him, so that when he maneuvered her attention, she followed like a lapdog, pivoting at his every unspoken command.

Well trained, I thought again, accidentally meeting his eyes a second time.

Could he tell what I was thinking? Did he look at me as a challenge—me with my Ketel One martini in hand and plate of rich appetizers at my side? When he nodded in my direction, giving me a sharp smile behind his date's back, was he seeing something to be tamed, something to be broken? I couldn't tell. I could only hope.

Near the end of the party, he made his way to my side and offered a hand in greeting. I took it, and we stood there, sizing each other up like athletes before a competition. There was a heat between us, palpable and real, and although I doubted even the possibility of a successful one-night love connection, I found myself dialing up the number for Rush the next week.

Just on a lark, I assured myself. Just to see.

Marlena was right. He liked pushing women. From the start, he had me out of bed three hours earlier than my usual demolishing of the alarm clock against the wall. Three fucking hours, I might say. I balked at the five A.M. appointment, explaining that I'm often up until dawn working, but he assured me that I'd have far more energy after training with him than I'd ever had before. When I showed up bleary eyed with a to-go cup of rich dark coffee in hand, he tossed my half-finished cup in the trash and shook his shaved head, disappointed. Rather than arguing with him, I found myself wanting to show him that I could do it, that I had it in me. I took his gaze as a challenge.

At least, I did until he started the workout.

Nothing could have prepared me for the pain. Nor for the way he dismissed the pain with a little half-smile, as if he were immune. As if the screaming agony of my poor muscles were nothing more than a little twinge of discomfort. I would have quit after one set of crunches, but I kept hearing Marlena's voice in my head: *Sadist. He's a total sadist.*

Was he one outside of the gym? That's what I desperately wanted to know.

So I played along, and I found myself striving harder to win his approval. When he shot a disparaging look at my battered gray pants, I traded those beloved college sweats for a pair of fitted black Lycra leggings. When he sarcastically queried how I could still be alive based on my irredeemable choices of food, I followed his carefully prepared diet, forgoing my favorite comfort meals for stone-cut oatmeal, freshly grilled wild salmon, egg-white omelets with baby spinach. I started to feel the burn, started to actually understand the concept of a runner's high. And I thought I felt something else, as well. When he trained me, his hand would linger on the small of my back, on the inside of my thigh, or on the curve of my waist. He'd position me just so, and then the professionalism would fade, and I'd feel a squeeze, or a touch or the softest pat.

Was it encouragement only, or was he interested?

Something in me started to change. Yes, I was crushing on this man, but I also became enamored of the sensations ricocheting through me. I did have more energy. He was right about that. Dark, smoky clubs started to feel just like they looked: dark and smoky. Why would anyone want to be trapped in one of those

places rather than spend hours in a clean, well-lit, healthy environment in the company of other clean, well-lit, healthy
people? My skin glowed. My brown eyes were brighter than
they had been in years. Friends noticed a change in my appearance, and I noticed that my clothes started to fit me differently.
I've always been slim. Now, I was hard. Addiction set in before
I was truly aware of what had happened.

I began going to the gym on days Granger wasn't training
me, just to work out on my own—amazingly finding that I truly
missed it if I skipped a day. And when I watched him from the
elliptical machine, surreptitiously viewing the way he behaved
with other clients, I realized that he didn't seem to touch the
other women the way he touched me—his fingertips light, the
tingle of sweat and lust keeping me ever off balance. He main-
tained a distance with the others that I reveled in. It was me he
was interested in. *Me* he wanted.

Finally, at the end of one session, he bent to whisper in my
ear, "We'll have a night lesson next."

"Night lesson?"

"Meet me here at eleven."

The gym closed at ten. This was going to be different. This
was what I'd been waiting for. I knew it. And I was right.

He didn't do anything out of the ordinary at first. Nothing
noticeable, anyway. He didn't tell me to strip out of my clothes
so that he could work me out naked, or whisper that he wanted
to fuck me up against the red vinyl slanted board, the site of my
countless nightmarish sit-ups. Instead, he moved me through my
regular routine, perhaps being slightly stricter than usual, forcing me to hold the weights longer, to breathe slower.

But then, as we neared the end, as my heart raced and my
blood pumped at a rapid pace, he put one strong hand on my
thigh. My whole body quivered at his touch. His fingers slid

between my legs, pressing against my Lycra-clad pussy as I lowered the gleaming silver barbell.

"Don't stop," Granger hissed, and I took a breath and forced
myself to do yet another rep. And another. This time, his fingertips slid in a smooth circle, touching my clit as I trembled
all over. I watched his eyes in the mirror, rather than my own.
Their blue was arctic, icy, and they froze me to my place.

"Concentrate," he insisted. "Come on, girl. Don't slack off
now."

A hiss of air escaped from between my clenched teeth.

"Don't look at me, baby—" *Baby. He called me baby. Like
all my other hard-core lovers. Like the men in black leather, not
black Lycra.* "—watch yourself."

With effort, I met my own gaze in the mirror and I did my
best. One, two, three, four, five, up. Then four beats down, a
little faster.

"Do it again, darling. Do it again."

Darling now, was it? *Darling* and *baby* and my muscles were
shaking uncontrollably. This was like being tied down. This was
like fucking on the floor of my tiny apartment. This was like a
belt in the air—

"Don't let me down."

No, I didn't want to let him down. Not now. Not ever.

One, two, three, four—oh, god, he was touching my clit just
right. So nice. My arms were trembling. His eyes were like ice
in the mirror, frozen blue. Colder than cold. *Don't stop. Don't
stop concentrating.*

He was training me. Training me in a whole new way. And
this was something I could understand. *These* were the lessons
I'd longed for.

We continued back at his apartment. He didn't change the
method of his training. He only changed the genre. His voice

was that same, fierce bark. His eyes held that same disapproving look when I failed to properly complete a task. Only now, we were alone. There were no others to see my downfall. No mirrors to reflect my transgressions into dizzying infinity. Now, he punished me in different ways. Not by forcing me to do an extra rep when my muscles were already screaming in agony—but by forcing me to bend over the sleek desk in his home office, to grit my teeth and wait for the sting of his leather belt on my naked skin.

He was a sadist. That was the truth. But I'd never known a sadist could live outside of the world that I inhabited. I hadn't known there were healthy vegan sadists; that there were men who knew how to take charge who didn't ride Harleys or hot rods, who didn't sport tattoos or scars from long-ago wipeouts.

Granger was one. He proved all my stereotypes wrong. And in a month, he had me well trained.

Trained to come when he called.

Trained to crawl across his apartment on my hands and knees. Trained to lower my eyes when he spoke my name in a certain tone. Trained to climax when astride his lap, facing my own reflection as he thrust his greased-up cock into my asshole, his fingers strumming my tender clit so that we reached our limits together.

His body was unbelievable. He could pick me up, position me, hold me exactly how he wanted to—just like that other gym rat so long ago. But this was different. I wasn't a weight to be pressed. I was a force to be possessed, a tangible energy to be bent and molded.

When we worked out together in the gym, I thought about how it felt when he fucked me. When he fucked me, I thought about him forcing me to do another crunch at the gym. "One more, baby. Come on, just one more." The two actions became synonymous in my head: working out and fucking. Being worked out and being fucked. On a solo run through the Hollywood Hills, I imagined him at my side, hissing orders, forcing me on past my limits, a leather belt doubled in his hand. In his bed, with my wrists cuffed tightly to the metal railing, I pictured myself doing another rep, always just one more rep, feeling my muscles shriek in protest, forcing myself to hit one more mark.

Both situations made me equally wet.

Granger had twisted everything up inside of me. Looking at my gym bag was foreplay. Staring at the weights he kept at home made me twist in my seat. I was ready for him all the time, but he liked waiting for it, forcing me through excruciating lessons before allowing himself to fuck me. He never seemed to lose his cool, even at our most heated moments. It was as if he had an icy core, one that showed only in his eyes and in his voice. He was never out of breath. Never mussed. Never shaken. I had faith in this quality of his. I bowed down before it.

"You're not trying," he said sometimes, and those were the words that made me feel the worst. All he asked from me was everything. I would have sweated blood to give to him. Whenever I questioned my abilities, I'd look into his eyes and find the strength to go forward. To prove myself to him. To win his praise.

I lost myself in the endorphin rush. I felt sleek and pure, given over both to the healthy attitude of being a gym rat, and the runner's high of being well trained.

And then, as athletics junkies occasionally do, I allowed myself to start to relax—both about my workouts and about my man. Granger was mine. I could tell. He was different with me. He was tender with me, even through the pain, or maybe *because* of the pain. Oh, was he tender.

I started to let down my guard, even to cheat every once in

a while. Cheat on the prescribed diet he'd written out for me, choosing an espresso over a white tea, a Reese's Peanut Butter Cup over a handful of hateful trail mix. I cheated on the intensity of my workouts, as well, stopping after two sets of ten reps rather than three, knocking off five minutes early when I was working out on my own. As if sensing this shift within me, Granger suddenly called to beg off my morning appointments. "This week's a bitch," he explained in his clipped tone. "I have to shuffle everything around to fit in a new client. Take a few days off. Give yourself a reward. Sleep in."

I did so for nearly a week, reveling in bad old habits. Letting sunshine wake me rather than the scream of an alarm. I expected my body to respond with glee—but it didn't. Instead, I looked at my forlorn gym bag with distress. Granger had trained me, and I had trained myself, to want to see sunrise when I left the gym, sweaty and happy, vibrating with the swirl of endorphins. So after five days off, I decided to show up predawn, as I had for so many weeks previously. I missed the way my body had ached all day. I missed the blinding pain that came right before the pleasure.

When I walked in the gym it was like walking in on two lovers. Surrounded by that healthy, brightly lit glow, the mirrored walls, the highly polished equipment, I felt my heart throb in my chest, as if I had just completed a ten-mile run when all I'd done was catch his eye in the mirror.

Sadist.

Marlena had said it. But she hadn't known. Hadn't comprehended.

Sadist.

I saw it. His blue eyes gleaming. His muscles pumped.

His hand on someone else's thigh.

TOO DIRTY TO CLEAN

I'm not supposed to be calling you.

Maybe that's why I'm so damn wet. The concept of doing things I'm not supposed to turns me on. Crazy, but I didn't learn that simple, sinful fact until I met you. I lived my whole life up to this point believing that being good had its own rewards. I shook my head in dismay as I watched friends wander down the back alleys of life, and I judged them internally, smugly pleased with myself and how well I went about my own business with no soap opera dramas.

Now, I know better. From you, I've learned that bad girls truly do have all the fun—which is fine, because I've crossed the line. I'm as bad as I can possibly imagine. This evening, my panties are sticky and clinging to me, and I am extremely aware of that dangerous heat and wetness at my center, and I know that I will get no relief. Not tonight, anyway.

Because I'm *really* not supposed to be calling you. I'm supposed to be on my way to the corner grocery store, to pick up something I forgot today when I did the rest of the week's shopping. That was the excuse I gave, anyway. Lame though it may sound, it was all I could come up with through the hazy, horny fog of my X-rated thoughts. *Need tomato paste for the sauce. It won't taste as good without. So be right back, honey.* But "right back" isn't supposed to include a stop at a graffiti-tagged pay phone around the corner, where I slide in two silvery quarters, dial your number from memory, and tell you how much I miss you.

And how much I miss your cock.

"Say that again," you prompt.

"Cock," I repeat automatically. "I miss your cock—"

"Tell me more. What do you miss the most?"

"I miss bending over, parting my thighs, and taking it."

"Taking—"

"Your cock," I say again, and I hear the low chuckle catch at the back of my throat as some sane part of my inner critique witnesses me having this unbelievable conversation. I manage to shock myself with the words that come automatically to my lips when you and I are on the phone. Or in bed together. Or outdoors at some semisecluded spot where we think we're safe. Where we think we're hidden—even though there is no real privacy in Los Angeles. Someone can always see you. That doesn't stop me from talking dirty. Because with you, I'm vulgar and I say things I wouldn't say in my other life. My real life. Where people think I'm good and kind and sweet and honest. With you, I say things that are darker, that cut closer to the bone. More importantly, I say things that are true. There's no need for false niceties, for faux conversational chatter. We don't have the inclination, and we don't have the time to fuck around. When we're together, we only have the time to fuck.

"Where are you?" you ask me now, and I know that you can

hear the annoying traffic sounds of Beverly and La Brea, and I'm certain that you can picture exactly where I am, and how it must feel to be where I am—in *both* the mental and physical locations.

"You know—" I say.

"Tell me," you insist. "Tell me, bad girl. Where are you?"

"Pay phone."

"Which pay phone."

"Down the street from our house."

"Our," you repeat caustically, just to drive that point home. It's not *ours* as in yours and mine, it's ours as in mine and *his*. "Don't want to chance the number on your cell phone?"

I don't answer. I don't have to. Yet I understand perfectly well what you are doing. You want me to revel in it—the lies and the cheating, the sneaking out to make a simple phone call. If I'm going to do this, then you're making me do the wrong of it right. Every guilty moment. Every stolen embrace. You have nothing to lose, so you can play all the mental mind-fucking games you want. I have everything to lose, on some far distant level, but at times like this, I'm amazed to find that I don't care. I'd trade it all in at this moment to be with you, but when I say that, you pounce, ready for me.

"Then why don't you call me from your place," you tease, "or have me over for dinner?" and I imagine you in your bed, naked, one hand pumping your cock. You've told me before that you can come just to the sound of my voice. I don't have to talk dirty. I don't have to do anything except say words—any words—and your cock throbs. I could make you come by reading the telephone book aloud, by reading dictionary definitions, by reciting poetry in Latin. We have that kind of connection. The right one to have with the wrong guy. Or with the right guy, at the wrong time.

And you are the right guy. You are the one guy, the only guy, who has ever made me feel sexy in my own skin. Sexy when I walk across the room naked. Sexy when I push myself off of your sweaty body and look around the floor for my discarded clothes. I get wet when I think about you. I squirm in my jeans, and I feel the arousal start. Just by picturing your eyes when you look at me, when you don't have to tell me what you want, when I just know. Or the way you grab onto my hair when we fuck. Your fist wrapped around my ponytail, pulling hard. Hurting me. Making me arch my back and lift my chin, making me stare in the mirror over your bed and see myself. See what a cheat looks like. What a slut and a tramp and—

"How long have you got?" you ask.

"Not long enough to come over."

"But long enough to get me off—"

I've come while astride your cock. Pushing up to gain leverage and then sliding right back down to the base. That had never happened to me before—coming while fucking without any help. Without the added assistance of my hand or my partner's hand on my slippery clit, teasing and stroking. I thought I must be in love with you for that to have happened. But you saw what I was thinking and you just grinned at me and shook your head. We have that connection.

That white-hot fucking connection. When I see you, I just want to take off my clothes and bend over. Or lie down. Or straddle you. I want to suck you off, or spread my legs and let you lick in sweet circles around my clit. I want to pump my hand up and down your cock, jacking you off.

All I want to do is fuck you.

But it's not so simple. I don't know why or how I got to this point. This grown-up place where I'm supposed to do the right thing. What I know is that it's not easy. I never thought I'd be crossing the line that I've crossed with you. I never thought I'd relate to all those clever songs: "The Dark End of the Street." "Slip Away." Christ, even "Hurts So Good." They're all about you and me. About what I want to do with you and what you're going to do with me.

"What are you wearing?" you ask next, and I look down, blushing at my lack of self-awareness, to see that I have no idea. I'm only thinking about you, and what you'd do to me if I could steal away tonight for long enough to let you. You'd be on me before I even shut your apartment door. You'd shred my clothes off me, push me up against the white plaster of your living room wall, and you'd fuck me so that I could feel it. Shaking me from the inside out. I'd grip into your skin, use my mouth to search for purchase on the strong ridge of your shoulder, bite you and mark you since you can't leave marks on me. I'd cry out loudly when I came. So loud and fiercely that it would sound as if I were in pain. Pleasure/pain. That's what it is.

I don't have it with him. He wouldn't pull my hair. He wouldn't slap my face or pinch my nipples until I cried out from that sharp spark of pain. He wouldn't put me over his lap and spank me, or push hard on my shoulders to make me kneel before him so that I could suck him off. Even if I asked, he wouldn't do those things to me. Instead, he'd get a disgusted look on his face and ask me where I could ever have come up with such a seedy idea. The same look I won from him when I suggested we check into a cheap motel sometime for a night of tawdry sex. The same expression I received when I asked him to fuck my ass. "Please," I begged. "I want to know what that's like."

The hypocritical thing is that it's not as if the thought itself troubles him. I know he's done it before. Early on, he told me so when we were at that share-everything point in our relationship.

You show me yours and I'll show you mine. So I know full well that he ass-fucked his ex-girlfriend Toni. Long time ago, sure, but he's done it. Yet he won't do it with me. There are things you just don't do with the girl you're going to marry. According to him, that is. According to his beliefs, there are ways you don't play with the mother of your future children. So he won't do those things with me.

You will.

You don't have any preconceived notions of who I'm supposed to be. Or why I shouldn't behave in a particular way. If I were to come to your house tonight, sneak away for longer than expected, you'd make me tremble simply by eyeing my body. By gazing at me with your jaw set, as if you were trying to decide which part to devour first. Which part to tie up, or spank, or fuck. Which part to bend over, or kiss, or shoot your cum on. But you'd choose after a moment's contemplation, and whatever you chose would make us both climax. Because you know me. You know me so fucking well that I don't even have to think when we're together. I just put myself in your hands and let you guide us.

So I'm well aware of the fact that when we were finished, for the first time, at least, you'd take me to the shower and scrub the sin away, and then you'd press me up against the cool black tiles and fuck it right back in me.

Because deep down inside, we both know what *he* doesn't know:

I'm way too dirty to clean.

YEAH

Do you ever think about fucking someone else?"

He asks it quietly, casually, as if the concept has just occurred to him. His fingers trail over my hip and then move lower, so that the very tips of his fingers graze my naked pussy lips. He bites hard into my bare shoulder, making me squirm, and then he croons the words again. "Do you, baby? Do you ever fantasize about making love to someone else?"

He wants me to tell him—he *thinks* he wants to know—but I know better. Questions like this are loaded. So of course, I just grin and half-shrug, and moan out the pleasure that I get from his touch. I don't give away my secrets so easily.

But yeah. Yeah I do. Doesn't everyone?

I think about the handsome green-eyed man who sits at the counter at the one good cafe in town. I'm always there with my little family, and he's always there all by himself. Every Sunday morning at 8:30. All by himself with the paper. He's older than me by far, silver-haired and well-worn in his jeans and his turquoise corduroy shirt. But he's good looking in that tough cowboy sort of way, and he's strong and straight backed, and I watch him drink his black coffee and read the paper, and I think about him.

I dress better than I need to for Sunday mornings at 8:30, putting a little extra effort into my outfit. I make an effort, and I think he notices. I think he knows I'm dressing for him. When we walk into the cafe, he always looks my way, and I see him memorizing the way I look, as if storing up my image for later use. At least, I hope that's what he's doing.

Sometimes, I imagine what I might say if we were to find each other all alone together. Maybe back by the pay phones near the two tiny restrooms. I try to picture our conversation, try to hear it in my head. Could I tell him I have such a crush on him? No. No fucking way. Not in a small town like this.

So instead, I fantasize. I think about him sliding me a note that tells me where and when to meet him. Someplace safe. Someplace close. I think about him taking off my carefully prepared outfit, my polished black boots, crisp jeans, white long-sleeved shirt. I close my eyes and feel his hands on me, stroking me, playing with my long dark hair. Then I think about the first kiss, and what it would feel like, and what it would mean. And after that first kiss, I think about him pushing on my shoulders, forcing me down to my knees, and watching me as I undo his fly and free his cock. I think about him grabbing my hair and pulling me forward, hard, so that I just barely have time to open my mouth before his cock slams down my throat. I think about sucking him hard, sucking to the very root of his cock, deep-throating him to show how much I want him, how much I want to give him pleasure with my mouth. And I do. I want to make him come, want to swallow every drop of him down. I think about him taking his cock out of my mouth, jacking it in his hand while I watch jealously. I think about him rubbing his cock against my cheeks, slapping my face with it, before sliding that length back down my ready throat.

"Do you ever think about fucking someone else?"

Yeah. Oh, god, yeah.

I think about the roughness of his skin against the softness of mine. I think about the way he watches me when I enter the cafe, the way he carefully gazes at me over the top of his paper, never smiling, yet fully acknowledging that he knows what I know—we both think about each other.

Fantasize, I should say.

Because I can see it in his eyes. I can see that he thinks about me when he comes, and this is what makes me dress a little better, and walk a little straighter. The thought of him jerking off to an image of me is what makes me touch myself late at night. That image blends to an action-picture of him fucking my mouth, of him using me. I can see this so clearly: I'd be naked; he'd be clothed, his jeans split open at the front, his hands so tight on me, gripping me, holding me.

I can feel his cock slipping back and forth between my lips, thrusting hard and forcefully into my mouth, and I know somehow that it would be good. Sex like that with him would be everything I think it would. Hard and quick, so that we could breathe again. Fast and furious with a vicious yet delicious climax, his hands on my shoulders leaving marks on me, bruising me with the intensity of his caress.

It's my number-one fantasy, sucking off this stranger. My favorite bedtime tale that I tell myself again and again. I change the location. I change the position. But the story is always the same. Me on my knees for a man whose name I don't know, letting him take his pleasure from me.

I make myself come every time to these thoughts, my body squirming, my hips rising, and in my head I see myself going up to him and saying a slightly altered version of the query my lover asks me: "Do you ever think about fucking me?"

But I don't have to do that.

I know exactly what his answer would be.

TEN MINUTES IN THE EIGHTIES

For ten minutes in the eighties, I was beautiful.

I've been beautiful since, but never like that.

Never again.

Before those magical ten minutes took place, I not only *wasn't* beautiful, I was hardly noticeable. Simply put, I was just another lowly freshman at UCLA, one of forty thousand others who called the campus home. Shy, insecure, terrified—those three adjectives fit me perfectly. In a land of voluptuous vixens and bottle blondes, I had no idea that with my sleek build and darkly mysterious features, I was far more than pretty. It never occurred to me that men would—and did—find me attractive or that all of the things girls lie awake at night and hope will happen to them would eventually happen for me.

Rather than put myself in a position to be rejected, I didn't give the guys a chance to approach. I kept my peers at a safe distance by creating an impression of constant motion. I hurried to class, spent hours studying in various libraries around campus, and used my free time cultivating miscellaneous interests as a deejay at the college station and a flunkey on the student paper. I was a good girl all year long, until the end of spring finals, when I finally let down my guard and got drunk with the rest of the students on my dorm floor. With no prior drinking experience, I downed five beers in one hour, and wound up, to the great surprise of my dorm mates, making snow angels on the cool turquoise and white tiles of the bathroom floor. Five beers will knock out any lightweight. And at five foot three, and 105 pounds, I was a lightweight.

In the morning, I experienced my first-ever hangover. For hours, I lay on the slim twin bed and stared at the ceiling, willing the rushing sound in my head to subside. When I eventually took a chance at walking upright, I realized that I'd missed the cafeteria's sole Saturday daytime meal. If I wanted to eat, I'd have to wait until six P.M., or fend for myself. Miserable, but yearning for sustenance, I took a taxi a mile off campus to the nearest grocery store. For a long time, I wandered aimlessly up and down the aisles, filled with an overpowering craving for something, *anything*, but not knowing precisely what. After choosing two items with the care that some women use when buying expensive jewelry, I took my place in line at the checkout. My self-prescribed day-after cure was a bottle of tomato juice and a can of Pringles (the only things in the whole store that seemed even mildly appealing).

It was while I was standing there with my red plastic basket in hand that I started to become beautiful.

I didn't know the transformation was happening right away. All I knew was that the handsome, dark-haired, forty-something man next to me in line was staring at me, his head angled so that he could look at me over his shades. I felt myself flush, pale skin turning scarlet, embarrassed because I had on the clothes I'd worn during the festivities the evening before, the clothes I'd ultimately slept all night in: faded blue jeans, a rah-rah-style university T-shirt in Bruin colors, and a thin navy blue hoodie. My turbulent raven curls had escaped from their standard ponytail, falling well past my shoulders to reach the middle of my back. Purple smudges of fatigue made my brown eyes look even darker than usual. I hadn't bothered with makeup of any kind.

Nervousness made me bite into my bottom lip. I felt overexposed beneath the fluorescent lighting and underprepared for a confrontation with a stranger. I tried to look extremely interested in the multitude of processed foods filling the fat woman's cart in front of me, but I felt the man staring relentlessly, and so I slowly turned to face him. As if encouraged by my action, he took a step closer to me, and in a low, soft voice, he whispered, "You have a look."

The way he said the words gave me an unexpected wave of confidence. Or maybe it was the lack of sleep talking. I don't know precisely why, but I met him head-on and said, "The drunken, slept in my clothes, barely post-hangover look?"

He shook his head. "That's not it. Something else. Something special."

I bit my lip again, harder this time. Here was a true Hollywood-style line, but I was no Hollywood starlet. Flustered and confused, I looked down at my white Keds, looked out the window at the half-filled parking lot, looked up at the bars of ugly lighting. Suddenly, it was my turn to pay for my groceries, and I fumbled in my pocket for my folded bills, then grabbed the change and my small paper bag of supplies and started to leave the store. The man abandoned his own few items on the gray conveyer belt and hurried after me.

"Where are you going?" he asked, his hand on my shoulder.

I didn't flinch away from him, but I pulled back, surprised by the power in his touch.

"Back to campus. I have a cab over there—" I gestured to the far corner of the parking lot. The blacktop glittered where shards of broken glass had melted into the oily asphalt.

"Tell him to go. I'll take you." He hesitated, as if he could sense the insecurity that had cloaked me for so many years, as if he could actually feel it. "Anywhere," he promised. "I'll take you. Wherever you need. Wherever you want to go."

I looked at him carefully. Here was the exact situation my parents had spent my entire teenage life worrying about and doing their best to protect me from. I was going to take a ride with a man I didn't know. And all their warding off of evil spirits did nothing to stop me. For some reason, I obeyed his command, paying off the cab and following him to the expensive, shiny silver sports car parked nearby. The car gleamed like foil in the bright sunlight.

"You should never accept a ride with a stranger," he told me severely as he opened the passenger door. "Especially a stranger in Los Angeles."

"I know."

"Then why are you choosing to ride with me?"

I smiled. I had been given the perfect answer. "You have a look," I said, and he laughed as he got into the driver's side and then slid an unmarked cassette into the tape deck. "I'm a music producer," he told me. "I just heard this tape for the first time. The boy's going to be huge."

It was Terence Trent D'Arby's *Introducing the Hardline According to...* and that music is embedded in my mind as a soundtrack to what happened next. The man drove me to his house high up in the Hollywood Hills where the movie stars live. He led me through the huge, well-decorated rooms, all the way to the mammoth patio in back. There, he gently took my clothes off my body and had me touch myself while he watched. And I was beautiful. For ten minutes in the eighties, I was so beautiful it was hard to handle.

I'd never done something like this before. Technically, I was a virgin. I'd had some kissing experience in high school, some backseat petting at a local drive-in theater, but shyness had kept me pure. Now, in the heat of the day, I touched myself while a stranger watched. I ran my hands over my body. I let my fingertips graze my nipples until they stood up hard and erect. I kept my eyes on the man as I let one hand wander lower, reaching to touch my pussy while he watched. The pool behind him was a true, aqua blue. The sky above matched that technicolor brightness. Standing there on the tiled deck, looking out at his multi-million-dollar view, I put on a show with my nakedness and my roving touch.

"That's right," he said, nodding, his voice hoarse as if he were as surprised by my actions as I was. "Do that."

He was seated on a deck chair, with his hands on his thighs, his sunglasses low down on his nose so he could look at me over the rim. I felt power in being naked. Felt a power in the way he drank in every touch of my fingertips on my stripped-bare skin. It was as if he were touching me, as well. When my fingers found the wetness coating my lips, he sighed before I did. I closed my eyes and leaned my head back, arching my slim hips forward, running my hands over my hip bones. The tiles were hot under my bare feet. The air was still and clear. My hair tickled against my naked back. My eyelashes fluttered against my cheeks.

I knew that he wouldn't touch me. Not unless I invited him to. Not unless I asked. But I didn't. I didn't need anything from him except his gaze. Because the way he stared at me—that's what did it. That was the magic that made me beautiful. I used my fingers to spread my nether lips wide apart. I ran my thumbs up and down over the ridge of my clit, first my right thumb, then my left, then both together, vying for control, until I knew that I was seconds away from coming. I touched myself harder, my eyes closed tighter, my whole body flexed as I waited for the change to take me away.

My mind was filled to bursting with images. I saw myself relaxing with a beer the night before, letting my guard down for the first time ever. I saw myself the way this man must have seen me, unwound, let loose from the tight confines I'd kept myself in all my life. I saw myself opening up, from the split of my body, from the cages within. This picture of freedom brought me to the brink. For me, there was nothing more freeing than standing naked in front of a total stranger—a man whose name I didn't even know—and letting him see everything.

He said, "Oh, god," when I came. He said the words for me, so that I didn't have to, and then, as if my pleasure had released him, he took off his sunglasses and came closer, on his knees on the patio, so very close to me, but he still didn't touch me. "Oh, Jesus," he said, as I brought my fingertips to my lips and slowly licked my own juices away.

"Don't stop," he said, and I knew from the sound of his voice that if I chose to, I could ask him for things. That he'd give me whatever I wanted. But all I wanted from him was his gaze. "Do it again," he said, "please make yourself come again."

With my fingers wet from my mouth, I parted my pussy lips for him, but this time, I slid two fingers deep inside myself. He was close now, his breath on my skin, and I pushed forward with my hips again, feeling his hair softly tickling against my naked thighs. I let him watch me from inches away as I fucked myself. I let him see everything, the way my clit grew so engorged with the heat from within. The way I worked myself hard with my fingers, thrusting my wrist upward against my body, slamming my hand inside me when the need grew stronger and then stronger still. I used only my right hand this time, my thumb rubbing back and forth over my clit, and when I felt the climax building, I put my left hand on his head and twined my fingers through his thick, dark hair, grabbing onto him, anchoring him as I came a second time.

"So beautiful," he said in that same low, steady voice. "You have this look, this goddamn beautiful quality. I knew when I first saw you—"

I picked up my clothes from around me on the tiles, and I dressed carefully, not hurrying. I felt as if I'd never hurry again, never be nervous again. When I was ready, he drove me back to my dorm, as he'd promised he would. Delivered me back in perfect condition, unmarred and unhurt, although I wasn't the same person. Not at all. I'd transformed under his gaze. I'd changed.

I guess sometimes that's all it takes, one person's gaze, one person's opinion, to make all the difference. Like the way he'd said that D'Arby would be big—a single person's opinion, summing up a powerful truth. It happens all the time in the media, the way it happened for me that time in L.A. In fact, just this weekend, I read a five-star review of Trent D'Arby's latest CD, and the reviewer wrote: *For ten minutes in the eighties, D'Arby was on top of the world.*

And for almost those same exact ten minutes, I was beautiful. For the first time in my life, I was so fucking beautiful it was hard to handle. Yeah, I've been beautiful since. But never like that.

Never again.

FOUR ON THE FLOOR

We weren't very nice about it. That was the surprising part. I expected the cliché of scented oils and the gilded candlelight ambiance and the slippery limbs entwined. But how we acted afterward was unforeseen. Alone together, reliving the night, Sam and I were truly cruel. And here I was, operating under a false impression for so many years.

You see, I always thought I was a nice girl.

Others reliving the experience might choose to focus on the way Sheila's gray-blue eyes had lit up when I'd pressed my mouth to her freshly shaved pussy, or the look on her husband Richard's craggy but handsome face as he started to slowly stroke his long, uncut cock. But not this girl. The best part of the evening for me was the laughter with Sam afterward, giggling all the way home about the freaks we'd spent the evening with. The freaks we'd just fucked.

They were decades older than us, and richer by far, and

they'd run a charming ad at the back of the *Guardian*. Filled with dizzy anticipation, we met for drinks, to check out the chemistry factor. Sizing up potential fuck partners is a heady business. Nobody else in the trendy after-work bar crowd knew that we were responding to a personal. Not the cute curly-haired bartender. Not the female executives lined up against the wall like pretty maids all in a row. The thought of what we were actually there for made me giddy with excitement, and desire showed rather brightly in my dark eyes.

The woman said I was pretty. Her husband agreed with an anxious nod. All evening long, they looked at me rather than Sam, and I knew why. Sam is tough. He has short, razor-cut hair and a gingery goatee. If you were to meet him in a back alley, you'd offer him your wallet in a heartbeat. You'd beg him to take it, the way I beg him to take things from me every night.

The couple didn't understand Sam. So they talked to me instead.

"So pretty," the woman repeated. "Like Snow White."

I grinned and drank my cosmo, then licked my cherry-glossed lips in the sexiest manner I could manage, leaving the tip of my tongue in the corner of my mouth for one second too long. Iridescent sparkles lit up my long dark hair. Multicolored body glitter decorated my pale skin. I wore serpentine black leather pants and a white baby-T with the word *SINNER* screaming across the chest in deep scarlet. There was an unspoken emphasis on how young I was in comparison to the woman. She was holding firm in her midforties, while I was just barely getting used to being in my early twenties. Her entire attitude was both calculating and clearly at ease, obvious in the way she held court in our booth, in the way she ordered from the waiter without even looking up.

"Two Ketel One martinis, another cosmo, another Pilsner."

I was her opposite, bouncy and ready, a playful puppy tug-ging on a leash. More than that, I was bold from sensing how much they wanted us, and I was wet from how much I wanted Sam. When he put one firm hand on my thigh under the table, I nearly swooned against him. We'd be ripping the clothes off each other in hours.

After drinking away the evening, we made a real date with the rich couple for the following weekend, a date at their place, where they promised to show us their sunken hot tub, wrap-around deck, and panoramic view of the city. In cultured voices, they bragged to us about the gold records from his music-pro-ducing days, and her collection of antique Viennese perfume bottles accumulated with the assistance of eBay. But although I listened politely, I didn't care about their money or what it could buy. All I wanted was all Sam wanted, which was simple: four on the floor.

We had done the act already, nearly a year before, with a low-er-class duo Sam found for us on the Internet. The woman was thirty-eight, the man twenty-six. They'd been together for two years, and had wanted to sample another couple as a way of en-hancing their already wild sex life. After dinner at a local pizzeria, and two bottles of cheap red wine, Pamela and I retreated to the ladies' room to show each other our tattoos. Hers was a dazzling fuchsia strawberry poised right below her bikini line. When she lifted her white dress, I saw that not only was she pantyless, but she'd been very recently spanked. She blushed becomingly as I admired her glowing red rear cheeks, where lines from Andy's belt still shone in stark relief against her coppery skin.

"He gave me what-for in the parking lot," she confessed. "Told me that he wanted me to behave during dinner."

"What would he think of this?" I asked, stroking her still-warm ass with the open palm of my hand.

"I think he'd approve," she grinned.

I gave her a light slap on her tender skin, and she turned around and caught me in a quick embrace, lifting my dress slowly so that she could see my own ink.

Teasingly, I turned to show her the cherries on my lower back, then pulled down my bikinis to reveal the blue rose riding on my hip. She traced my designs with the tips of her fingers, and I felt as if I were falling. Her touch was so light, so gentle, and in moments we started French-kissing, right there in the women's room at Formico's, while I could only imagine what the men were doing. Speaking of macho topics to one another, sports and the recent war, while growing harder and harder as they waited for us to return to the red-and-white-checked table.

Sam and I followed the duo to their Redwood City apartment, and into their tiny living room, overshadowed by a huge-screen TV and a brown faux-leather sofa. Pamela had her tongue in my asshole before my navy blue sleeveless dress was all the way off, and my mouth was on Andy's mammoth cock before he could kick off his battered black motorcycle boots.

The TV stayed on the whole time we were there. Muted, but on. We had crazy sex right on the caramel-colored shag rug in front of it, while heavy metal bands played for us in silence. It was like doing it on stage with Guns N' Roses. Surreal, but not a turn-off.

I remember a lot of wetness—her mouth, his mouth, her pussy. I remember Sam leaning against the wood-paneled wall at one point in the evening and watching, just watching the three of us entwined, the TV-glow flickering over us, my slim body stretched out between our new lovers. I felt beloved as their fingers stroked me, as they took turns tasting me, splitting my legs as wide as possible and getting in between. I held my arms over my head and Sam bent down and gripped my wrists tight while Pamela licked at me like a pussycat at a saucer of milk.

Scenes flowed through the night, lubricated by our red-wine daze, and we moved easily from one position to another. Pamela bent on her knees at Sam's feet and brought her mouth to his cock. I worked Andy, bobbing up and down, and after he came for the first time, I moved over to Pamela's side, so we could take turns drinking from Sam. I was reeling with the wonder of it. The illusion that anything was possible. Any position, any desire.

"You like that?" Andy asked when I returned to his side, pointing to Pamela as she sucked off my husband. "You like watching?"

I nodded.

"What else do you like?"

"I like that you spanked her," I confessed in a soft voice.

"Ah," he smiled. "So you're a bad girl, too."

My blush told him all he needed to know, and soon I was upended over his sturdy lap, and the erotic clapping sounds of a bare-ass spanking rang through the room. Andy punished me to perfection, not letting up when I started to cry and squirm, making me earn the pleasure that flooded through me. Sam filled Pamela's mouth while watching another man tan my hide.

Andy was a true sadist, which I could appreciate. He had a pair of shiny orange-handled pliers which he used like a magician on his girlfriend's teacup tits. She didn't cry or scream; she moaned. He twisted the pliers harder, and her green eyes became a vibrant emerald, as if she'd found some deep hidden secret within herself, and as if that secret gave her power. Andy told us stories of how he liked to spank her with his hand or a belt or paddle. Sometimes he used a wooden ruler. Sometimes he used whatever was nearby. He told us detailed stories of how he fucked her up the ass; how he made her bend over and part her cheeks for him, holding herself open as wide as possible and begging him for it. He liked to lube her up good, and then pour a handful of K-Y into his fist and pump his cock once or twice before taking her. The size of his cock in her back door would often make her cry, but it was a good sort of cry, he explained. Pain and pleasure were entwined in everything they did. Andy's stories made me more excited, and we kept up our games all night long.

Sam and I had fun with that couple, and we didn't laugh afterward. We fucked. Not like bunnies, which are cute and soft and sweet. We fucked like us. Hard and raw and all the time. Sam's large hand slapped down on my ass, connecting over and over as he relived the night. "You little cock slut," he said, his voice gravelly and low. "Your mouth was all hungry for him. You couldn't get enough." I would be red and sore after our sessions, and I relished every mark, every pale plum-colored bruise, every memory. The night was fuel for a year's worth of fantasies. We got precisely what we wanted, even though we never saw them again, because the woman turned out to be mildly insane. She called and called after our one-night stand. She emailed that she was in love with me, that she was desperate to see me. But Sam and I didn't want love. We wanted something much less involved but much more momentarily intense: four on the floor.

With Sheila and Richard, we got a great deal more than we bargained for. A gourmet dinner—delivered by a local party service—that dragged on for hours. A tour of their two-story house and their walk-in closets. Close-up views of their his-and-hers Armanis. We received an in-depth explanation of how their pure pedigreed dogs, who were busy in the corner of the living room chewing on pigs' ears, had been "de-barked." Their voice boxes had been removed, which had caused the dogs so much trauma, the pets were now on puppy Prozac.

These appearance-obsessed people were the ones we were about to have sex with. I had a difficult time picturing it. Yes, she was attractive, although *cool* was a better word. Yes, I liked how distinguished he looked in his open-necked crisp white shirt and pressed khakis with the ironed crease down the center. He was so different from Sam with his faded Levi's and dangling silver wallet chain. But they were trying to win us over, and somehow that made me feel hard and bristly inside. Didn't stop us from getting busy, though—choosing a spot far away from those demented dogs and peeling our clothes off. Richard didn't fuck me. He sat nearby and stroked my sleek dark hair out of my eyes and said he wanted to watch. Sheila had on a black velvet catsuit, and she stripped it off with one practiced move and was naked, her platinum hair rippling over her shoulders, her body gleaming chestnut in the candlelight. She stood for a moment, holding the pose, waiting for applause or flashbulbs.

Sam took his cue from Richard at first, backing away, watching while Sheila courted me. Sheila had obviously done this before. She strode to my side and helped to undress me. She cooed softly, admiringly, as she undid my bra and pulled it free, as she slid my satin dove-gray panties down my thighs. Her fingers inspected me all over, as if checking to see that a purchase she'd made was acceptable. She kissed wetly into the hollow of my neck and caressed my breasts with her long, delicate fingers, tweaking my rosy nipples just so to make them erect. Then she spread me out on the luxurious multicolored living room rug and started to kiss along the basin of my belly. I had one second to wonder why it is that ménages never take place in beds before I sighed, arched my back, parted my legs for her, and closed my eyes. She turned her body, lowered herself on me, and let me taste her.

Everything about her body felt cool, like polished chrome. Her skin. Her lips. Her tangy juices when they flooded out to meet my tongue. We sixty-nined for the men, and for a moment, I was won over. I was fine, alert, and happy. With my mouth on the older woman's pussy, and my hands stroking her perfect silky body, I lost myself in momentary bliss. She was exotically perfumed, a scent I didn't recognize but knew must have been imported from Europe. She even tasted expensive. But sex levels out any playing field. I might only have been able to afford Cover-Girl dime-store cosmetics rather than Neiman Marcus special blends, but I could find her swollen clit easily, and that's all that mattered. I teased it out from between her perfectly shaved pussy lips. I sucked hard, and then used my tongue to trace ring around the rosy.

When I felt Sam's eyes on me, I turned my head to look at him. He gave me a wink, as if to let me know that he approved, and then he nodded forward with his head for me to continue. I could already hear his voice in my mind: "You liked your mouth all glossy with pussy juices, didn't you, girl? You liked the way she tasted, all slippery and wet?" But then Sheila started to direct, positioning my body on all fours, before grabbing a carved wooden box from under the coffee table and pulling out a variety of sex toys. This wasn't like Andy lifting his pliers off the oval-shaped coffee table, an unexpected turn-on. This was planned; I could tell. We had been carefully chosen to star in a prewritten fantasy of Sheila's. A fantasy in which she was the star and I was her assistant, her underling, her protégé. And even as she buckled on the thick, pink strap-on, I felt myself withdraw.

Still, we fucked.

FOUR ON THE FLOOR

She took me from behind, holding tightly to my long black hair, and rode me. Her well-manicured fingertips gripped firmly near the base of my scalp, holding me in place. Sam stared into my eyes as I was pounded by this icy woman, and then he came close, his cock out, and placed the head on my full bottom lip. I heard Sheila hiss something—Sam was taking charge and she didn't like it. But she also didn't know Sam. Sam would have none of her noise, the way she would have none from her dogs. He fucked my mouth fiercely while she fucked my cunt, and Richard, silent and somewhere off inside himself, tugged on his dick and watched us all.

Sheila had oils that she spread on me with the finesse of a masseuse, and soon we were drippy and glistening in the golden light. She had sturdy metal nipple clamps and assorted colorful dildos, vibrating devices, and butt plugs. She arrayed her collection and went to work. And Sam let it all happen. This was far different, and far less spontaneous, than our experience with Pamela and Andy, but we'd use it. We'd go with it. There were four of us, after all, and we were there.

I came when she oiled me up between my rear cheeks and slowly slipped in a petal-pink butt plug, her knowing fingers working between my thighs to tickle my clit as she filled my ass with the toy. I came again when Sam jacked himself hard and let loose in my mouth, filling me up with his cream as Sheila fucked me from behind. I jammed my fingers between my legs, working my own clit to come a final time when Richard, so distant, lowered his head and shuddered, his body wracked with tremors as he climaxed a white fountain up onto his hard belly.

But in the car on the way home at two A.M., still reeking of imported essential oils, still throbbing from the poundings I'd taken, I started to giggle. And then Sam started to laugh out loud.

"Voice boxes removed," he said, shaking his head as he drove along the empty highway.

"Crazy."

"So much Armani," he snorted.

"And gold records."

"And cigars."

"And their view."

"And their money."

And we didn't see them again, even though they called for weeks afterward. Even though they fell a little bit in love with us, as had Pamela and Andy. Because Sam and I weren't looking for love. We had plenty of that. We were looking for one thing only. And somehow I was sure that we'd find it again once I placed a personal ad of our own:

Happily married twosome seeks similar couple for debauchery. For intensity. For four on the floor.

WANNA BUY
A BIKE?

In Amsterdam, you can prove the Rolling Stones wrong. Here, you actually *can* always get what you want. That is, if what you want are drugs—any drugs—or sex—any sex. Sex with men. With women. Orgies. S/M. B/D. Name the perversion and you can make it come true.

Sure, I understand the benefits of having such readily available pleasures. In the States, you have to search out the seedier sides if you've got a taste for trouble. So I realize how someone might enjoy being able to walk down an alley, point to a window, and buy the person behind it for an hour of frisky fun. Yet the type of freewheeling environment found in Amsterdam poses a problem for girls like me. Girls who like the darker side of things.

The rush, I've always found, is in delving into that cloak-and-dagger ambiance and plunging down the steps into the unknown. What's illegal in Amsterdam? You can walk into a coffee shop and buy your marijuana, walk into a pharmacy and

purchase magic mushrooms. No need to skulk through alleys
after your personal yearning. For some, it's a fantasy come true.
But I fucking hate it.

This is why I was sulking miserably through a rainy Amsterdam afternoon, a scowl on my face, my long black hair
windswept, my eyes troubled. In each cozy cafe, college students
sent fragrant plumes of smoke toward the lazily spiraling ceiling fans. Content and flush-cheeked, the smokers slipped deeper
into their daydreams, looking as if they were right out of a
painting—Norman Rockwell for the new millennium.

In the red-light district, I knew I could find someone to take
care of whatever I craved, which made me crave absolutely
nothing. While others tightened their coats against the harsh au-
tumn storm, I rebelled in the only way I could, pushing back the
hood of my heavy black jacket, pulling open the buttons, letting
the water hit my skin.

The one thing I do love about Amsterdam is the setup of the
city: intricate circles and circuits of canals. Wet and pungent,
filled with houseboats, fallen leaves from gold-flecked trees,
ducks, and debris. I like the idea of the circles, one slipping
inside the other as they get closer to the center. Rings around
rings, like the spiraling efforts of a lover's tongue nearing the
bull's-eye of a woman's clit.

With thoughts like that on my mind, it was no wonder that I
was aroused. But I felt as if I were on the verge of coming without ever being able to reach the climax. Searching for something
unknown in a city where you can get anything as long as it has
a name and you have the price....

"Wanna buy a bike?" a voice asked as I rounded a corner,
breaking through my unhappy haze. Turning, I saw the first
evidence of the Amsterdam underground. A scruffy-looking
youth with tousled, birch-colored hair and a dead-eyed green

stare captured my attention. Handsome, but weathered about the edges, he had the look of someone who'd been up all night. It's a look that I find seductive.

"Excuse me?" I asked.

"Pretty girl," he beckoned, and I took a step further away from the crowds of tourists and into the mouth of the stone-cobbled alley where he stood. "Do you wanna buy a bike?"

And now I understood. Where, in any other city, this man would be offering me drugs or sex or something not easily found on the street, he was hawking bicycles instead. Good as gold in Amsterdam.

"Cheap," he added in perfect English. "With a seat and handlebars. Everything."

In Amsterdam, you have your choice of how to get around. You can walk—like I do—or use a trolley, a boat, a car (if you have balls of steel), or a bicycle. The problem, in my opinion, is that everyone is stoned on something, and they drive as if to prove that you can handle a vehicle while your mind is flying. Trolleys split pedestrians and make them scurry for safety. Bicycles cut off cars. I might trust myself on two wheels, but I wouldn't trust those around me. Still, the excitement of embarking on something illicit made me shift in my wet jeans. Danger is my all-time favorite aphrodisiac.

"Where is it?" I asked, looking around.

"Don't carry the product on me," he said tersely, and I thought I saw a sneer on his attractive face, as if he were thinking, *What can you expect from a foreigner?*

"How much?"

He leaned forward to quote the price, and I saw the way his eyes looked at me. As if he'd suddenly noticed that my jacket was open, my lipstick-red T-shirt wet and tight on my slim body, my jeans soaked through.

The price he quoted was high for a bike, but low to fulfill my need. I nodded, and he motioned for me to follow him, back down that alley to another. Quick-stepping as we made our way to some unknown destination, I heard the way my boots sounded on the walkway, that staccato beat, heard the echo of my beating heart in my ears. This was adventure, excitement, the reason I'd come to Amsterdam in the first place. And why was I getting all warm and aroused? Silly girl, silly girl. It was because I was about to buy a bike.

"This way," he urged, "just down that street."

I tried to keep up with him, but ended up walking behind, and that was okay. The rear view of this youthful dealer was something to be admired. Like me, he had no qualms about getting wet, and his Levi's were a dark ocean blue, tight on his fine ass, slicked down on his lean legs. He had on a black sweater, also drenched, and that unruly white-blond hair that seemed bed-rumpled instead of just plain wet.

When we got to our destination, he wanted the money. But I've made deals with street salesmen before. It's important to see the merchandise before you put up the cash, regardless of the country you're in.

"Don't trust me?" he asked, grinning, and I shook my head. "This way, then," he said, and we continued on our route, around one of the comeliest canals of the city, where even the ducks were now hiding beneath the arched bridges to get out of the cold driving rain. What did they have to worry about? They lived in water.

"Just a bit further," he said, and I wondered as I spotted a familiar-looking kiosk whether we were going in circles. Didn't matter to me. I'd have followed as long as he led. But soon he stopped again, this time in front of one of the skinny, gingerbread-colored houses that tour-leaders love to point out as the "charm" of Amsterdam. Chained to a railing was a shiny blue bicycle, just as he'd described. Two wheels. Handlebars. A seat. Everything.

"You believe me now?" he asked, and he took a step closer as he held out his hand for the money. His fingertips could have brushed my breasts through the tight, damp shirt, could have stroked the line of my chin, tilted my head up for a kiss. I felt my breath speed up, but I didn't let on. I can play as streetwise as I need.

"The key?" I asked, pointing to the bike lock, and the corners of his eyes crinkled at me as he smiled again. He seemed to have more respect for me now, sensed that I was willing to play any game he named.

"A little further," he said softly, turning on his heel and continuing the walk. *Such a smart-ass,* I thought. He'd have taken my money at the first place, then told me to wait while he got the bike, disappearing forever. At the second stop, where I could actually see *a* bike, he would have made more excuses—"I need to get the key"—and then vanished. Now, we were testing each other. Him to see if he could get the money from me. And me to see if he might sense something else that I wanted.

Once again, we were walking down another alley. At the end stood a long metal rack, with at least fifty cycles attached. The dealer nodded toward the mess of metal. "You choose one," he said, "tell me the color, and I'll get it for you. *Then* you pay."

"I'll need a lock, too," I said.

"Locks are no good. Watch what I do to one."

I looked over the rack of bikes and found one that I liked. "The emerald green."

He smiled. "Five minutes. Meet me back there," and he pointed down the alley to a bridge. "On the other side."

This was fine with me. If he didn't show up, I wasn't out

anything. If he did, well, we'd just see. For the first time, I felt happy to be in Amsterdam. The city *was* lovely, even rain-streaked, and the abundance of drugs and easy sex made the people around me seem at peace. Who *isn't* blissful when they've just gotten laid, or smoked a big fat one, or done both simultaneously?

At the meeting spot, I waited in the rain, shivering, and in less than five minutes he was there, wheeling the bike ahead of him. Now it was my turn to pull a fast one.

"I have to get the money," I said. His eyebrows went up and he frowned at me, but I shook my head quickly to reassure him. "I have it, but it's at my hotel," I told him, naming the location. My smile must have let him know what I was offering. More than payment for a bike. "Don't you trust me?"

"We'll ride there," he said. "It's quicker."

I found myself perched over the back wheel as we sped down the streets, cutting off taxis and trolleys, wreaking havoc with pedestrians, and then joining a sea of other cyclists until finally we were at my hotel. He carried the bike into the lobby for me, where the concierge promised to watch it. Then we headed up the stairs together, soaking wet, dripping little puddles on the carpet as we walked.

At my room, I paid him first, just in case that was really all he wanted. He took the money, folded it, and slid the bills into the side pocket of his jeans, just before he slid his jeans down his legs. Smiling, I stripped, as well, and soon we were naked together, pressed against the wall of my hotel room. Our bodies were wet and cold, at first, then wet and a little warmer as we created heat together.

I like sex. Especially unexpected sex. And this beautiful boy seemed perfectly ready to give me what I needed. He took his time. Starting with a kiss, he parted my lips with his, met my tongue, moving slowly, carefully. Then he grabbed both of my wrists in one hand and held my arms over my head, pinning me to the wall. With my wrists captured, he brought his mouth along the undercurve of my neck, then kissed in a silky line to my breasts. I arched my back, speaking to him with my body alone, making silent, urgent requests. He didn't fail me. First, he kissed my left nipple, then my right, then moved back and forth between them until I was all wet again. A different type of wetness from being soaked to the skin outdoors. Now, I was soaked within.

It was time for him to fuck me, and I wanted to say this, but I realized to my embarrassment that I didn't know his name. I felt a moment of panic, then decided it didn't matter. We had our agreement, our arrangement, and that bond of dealer to seller should have been all the information I needed. So I locked onto his clear green eyes and tilted my head toward the large bed in the center of the room. He grinned, lifted me in his arms, and carried me to it.

There was romance in the gesture that pulled at me deep inside, from the base of my stomach to the split between my legs. Even though I was the same girl who had gotten off in the past by being taken in public, being tied down with leather thongs, bound with cuffs, spanked with paddles, fucked with dildos. Kink has always tended to make me come. But this time was different.

The thrill, I have always found, lies in the unknown. Plunging down those steps into darkness has always been my favorite way to play. Yet, usually, the need for danger takes me into extreme situations. This time, I found myself on a normal bed in an average hotel room, doing something extraordinary with a stranger.

"Trust me," he said, and I nodded.

The boy spread me out on the bed and continued with his kissing games, making his way to the intersection of my body, then tracing a map of Amsterdam's canals around and around my clit. His tongue slid deep inside me, then pulled out, went back in to draw invisible designs on the inner walls of my cunt, and then out again, leaving me breathless and yearning.

"Now," I murmured, and he nodded, understanding. But then he moved off the bed again, rummaging through his pile of wet clothes until he found the bicycle lock and chain that he'd removed from my new cycle. Back at my side, he used the heavy metal links to bind my arms together over my head. No lock needed, just the chain wrapped firmly around my slender wrists. That was perfect, divine—just the type of rush that I craved.

Then, sitting up on the bed, he used his hands to part the slicked-up lips of my pussy, and his fingers slipped into my wetness. I sensed it a second before his cock pressed into me, and I stared into his eyes as we were connected. And, oh Christ, that feeling was almost overpowering, the length of his rod as he thrust deep inside me, following the same route made by his tongue moments before. Only now, I basked in the fullness of it. Thick and long, his cock filled me up.

Before I could even think about what I might want next, his fingers came back into play. He kept my pussy lips spread apart, stretching me open, and then the tips of his fingers began to tap out a sweet and unexpected melody over my clit. I sighed and ground my hips against him, letting him know how much I liked what he was doing. Then I squeezed him, from deep within, and this time he was the one to sigh. Open-mouthed, eyes wide and staring into mine, he watched me for the whole ride. Held me with a gaze so intense that I couldn't look away.

This sent me over the edge. His fingers, his eyes, his cock, his tongue all combining to take me there, to lift me up. To send me.

My body closed in on his, and then opened up, squeezing and releasing, bringing him right up there with me. Pushing him over.
"Beauty," he whispered, stroking my still-wet hair away from my face as I came.

When I went downstairs later in the afternoon, the bike was gone, of course.
"Your friend, he took it," the concierge told me with a smile. "But he left you this." The money was sealed in one of the cream-colored envelopes kindly provided by the hotel. Fair trade. He knew I didn't really have use for a bike in Amsterdam, and if he'd taken the cash, that would have made him a whore instead of simply a street dealer. It was a wholly complete transaction, and I knew that I should have been satisfied.

Still, the next day found me walking through the city with a mission, pausing at each darkened alleyway until I heard the words that made me wet.

"Hey, pretty girl," he whispered, his voice low and seductive, "wanna buy a bike?"

WHY CAN'T
I BE YOU?

Sounds silly, I guess, but sometimes when I see him, I don't want to fuck him, I want to *be* him. Matt has the perfect male body, in my opinion. Broad shoulders; a long, lean torso; slim hips; and an amazingly awesome ass. He has a deeply fuckable body, and I do love to fuck him. But sometimes I don't want him to climb on top of me and pound into me, don't want him to bend me over and take me from behind, don't want him to press me up against the wall and make me writhe with pleasure.

No, what I want is to slide inside him and see the world from within his head. And I want to devour some summertime chicklet dolled up in one of those swishy floral dresses and tie-up espadrilles and fuck *her* while being him.

Too much like *Being John Malkovich*?

Maybe.

But why can't I be him? Just for an evening. Or even for an hour. Why can't *I* be the one to move through the crowd and pick up a girl, any girl? (He can have any girl.) Why can't I take one home, or out to some back alley, and push her up against the brick wall out there, tear her panties down and fuck her?

That's all I want. One hour. One hour inside of his body so that I can find out what it's like—not just to be a man, but to be *him*. I want to manhandle my throbbing cock, to hold it, to fondle it. I want to force-feed every inch of it to some pretty, summertime chicklet, to make her drink me, and drain me. To make her feel my power.

He's not always that type, I know. He is sweet and caring and gentle. He is monogamous and dedicated to me. But *I'd* be that type if I were him. I'd be the type to control the situation. I'd be the type to take charge. It would feel good to take charge. God, it would feel amazing.

I get to the point where I am all-consumed by the idea. So I take one step forward, or really one roll forward on the mattress, and I curl my body up next to his in bed, and I say, "I have a fantasy...."

He slides one strong arm around me, holding me close. "Tell me, baby," he whispers back, the way he always does. He likes my mind best. More than my ripe, lush breasts. More than my thick, black hair. More than the curves of my hips or the swell of my ass, he likes my thoughts. My dirty fantasies. My X-rated visions. "Tell me where your mind is going tonight," he croons in his low, husky voice.

"I want..." I start, but I can't say it.

"Tell me."

"No," I whisper, shaking my head.

"Tell," he says, and his voice is insistent.

"I'll show you," I decide. Because that will work best.

"Show—" he starts, but I put my finger to his lips, and without another word, I climb out of bed and grab the satchel containing my outfit and all my recently purchased gear, and I disappear into our bathroom. I can almost hear his thoughts going crazy in the other room—*Where is she going? What's she doing?*—but I pay more attention to my own thoughts. At this point, they're all that matter.

I gaze at myself as I bind my breasts flat with an Ace bandage. I admire my body as I slip into the recently purchased harness and adjust my fine, handsome cock. I slide into the faded 501s, and put on the boots, and add a wife-beater T-shirt that makes my arms look cut and fierce.

Who am I?

Will he know?

I gel my hair and tuck my ponytail up into a cap, then slip on a pair of his shades. I can see it. I can feel it. I add cologne, from the expensive bottle I bought him last Christmas, and then I walk back into our bedroom and wait to see what his response will be.

"Oh, Jesus," he sighs when he sees me, and I know with that ripple of pleasure that runs instantly through me that he's game. "Oh, *god*," he says, looking me up and down. I'm tall and lean and hard. My hand is already on my belt. I want to undress as quickly as I wanted to dress. But first, I have to strip him down. I have to oil him up. I have to kiss him all over, lovely flower that he is. Because now that I'm him, well, who does *he* have to be?

We don't need to answer that question, do we? I didn't think so.

Even though I feel like being naked so he can really see the transformation, I don't take off my clothes this time. I need him too fast for that. I part my jeans and let him admire my cock. I manhandle my cock, my fist wrapped tight around it. I want to slide it across his pretty lips. I want to watch him deep-throat it.

He wants that, too.

"Look," I say. "Get close so you can see me. Really see me."

He scrambles on the bed to obey. His mouth is open before I can command it. I don't have to tell him what to do. His lips part, and he takes me in. I feel him pulling on my cock. I feel how hungry he is for that. I envision him draining me, taking me all the way to climax with the sucking motions of his ravenous mouth.

Later. *After.*

For now, I push him back. There's lube in the drawer by the bed. Usually, it's lube for me. Now, it's lube for him. I tell him to get me the bottle, and then I let him watch me grease myself up.

"You know where this is going," I say, seeing his eyes widen, seeing him bite hard on his bottom lip, as if he might want to say something, but doesn't quite dare. "You know," I say, softer, but I can tell from the rosy blush on his face that he understands. Of course he does. Then I roughly roll him over on the bed, and pull his boxers off, and spread those lovely asscheeks of his, and kiss him there between them. *Mmm.* I take my time, the way he takes his time, and I can tell as he grows more aroused from the way he shifts against the sheets.

He likes this. My baby likes this.

I oil him up, so gently, so sweetly, my fingers going deep inside of him, and while my fingers work slowly into his asshole, I press my face against his smooth skin and breathe in deep. Oh, is he sweet. He is my angel. My lover. My sweet young thing in a floral dress and tie-up espadrilles, so ready and willing to get fucked against some back-alley wall.

I sit up on my haunches, and I get ready to plunge. My baseball cap comes off, but my hair stays in place, and I'm still him as I work the first part of my thick, ready cock into his asshole.

And as I fuck him, I realize that we've blurred, because there I am in the mirror. There I am. But who am I? And there he is, his expression one of awe and surrender. And who is he? And more important than either of those questions is this one: Does it matter?

No. Not at all.

Not tonight.

CALIFORNIA DREAMING

Alden wanted to watch another man fuck me.

You just can't say it any plainer than that.

As he rolled me over in bed, parting my long legs and sliding his cock deep inside me, he whispered his favorite fantasy. "Just once," he assured me. "Oh, baby. Just one time. I know what you're like in bed. I know how you feel, and how you look, and how you taste. But I want to watch another man learn those sexy secrets. I want to see you come while he takes care of you."

"He?" I asked.

Doggie-style lets Alden go in deep, and for a moment, he couldn't respond. But even though I was as turned on as my man, I wouldn't let up, waiting only a moment before murmuring more insistently, *"He?"* as I gazed into the mirror above our bed and stared at our reflections. Alden is dark-haired and bronze-skinned, with gray-green eyes that sheen with an insatiable sexual appetite.

"You know who—" Alden said, slamming faster now, really fucking me. I slid one hand between my legs and touched my clit, fingering myself gently as Alden continued, "You *know*, baby. The pool guy."

Oh, god. The pool guy.

Alden and I rent a large, Spanish-style bungalow in sun-drenched Santa Monica. The best part about the house is the backyard pool—a lush aqua gem in a lagoon setting. And the best part about the pool is the stunning man who comes once a week to clean it. Talk about your California dreaming.... Will is tall and long-limbed, with blond hair and eyes that rival the blue of the deep end of our oval pool. When I first saw him, I felt that naughty pang you get when you're in a long-term relationship and notice a particularly beautiful specimen.

Although I've never been much of a swimmer, I instantly began to fantasize about taking a decadent dip into the pleasurable waters of sex with Will. Now that I'd been given free rein to enjoy these fantasies, they came more and more often. In bed, in the shower, in line at the grocery store. Whenever I closed my eyes, that vision awaited me. I was California daydreaming, in a constant state of enhanced arousal. Somehow, though, the naughtiness didn't disappear even though these fantasies were green-lighted by my man. Because Alden wasn't suggesting a threesome, where he might go out and have a beer with Will at the tapas bar around the corner, explain the sex-charged situation, then casually invite him into our boudoir—no, he wanted to watch, surreptitiously watch, while I got it on with the pool guy.

And the thing of it is, nothing had ever excited me more.

"Here's the deal," I explained to my boyfriend after many pleasurable fantasy sessions. "I don't want to plan this to death. If it happens, it happens, otherwise, we can forget about it. This isn't something I'm willing to force."

That was good enough for Alden—and as it turned out, he didn't have to wait long. Next week, when Will arrived, I knew what to do. I walked by the pool in my indecently short white robe and settled myself on one of the outdoor wood-and-canvas lounges, as if I were innocently positioned there to catch a few mid-afternoon rays. Alden was upstairs in his office, and I knew that if he looked out through the blinds he'd be able to see everything.

"Hey," Will said to me, quickly glancing up from his job.

"Hey," I said back, untying my white terry-cloth robe and letting it fall open. I wasn't wearing anything underneath. Not a string bikini. Not a skimpy thong. With my shades on, I pretended to completely ignore Will, but I knew he wasn't able to do the same with me. No straight man could have. His eyes were focused on the silky expanse of skin showing in the parting of the robe. I could almost feel him grow hard from where he stood.

After a few minutes, he walked to my side of the pool, then to my side of the lounge, and finally he sat down right at the edge.

"You're going to burn," he said, reaching for the suntan lotion.

"You mean it's going to get so hot?"

He looked at me, eyebrows raised.

"You know," I smiled, shaking the robe off completely. "When we fuck—"

That's all the encouragement he needed. But before we continued, I reached into the pocket of my robe for a condom.

"You're prepared," he grinned.

"Like you wouldn't believe."

"And what does Alden think about all this?" he asked, as he rolled on the condom.

"We have an arrangement..." I whispered.

"Oh," he breathed, "an *arrangement.*"

His hands were rich with the oil and he slid them up and down my naked body. I breathed in deep to catch the tropical scent of the oil mixed with the bougainvillea growing on the stucco and the sweet honeysuckle way at the back of the yard. I sighed and arched, and Will rolled me over and pressed me down on the towel, his shorts open, his body on mine.

I visualized Alden watching every move. I could see it in my mind as he pressed himself up to the blinds, one firm hand on his rigid cock, tugging as he watched Will enter me from behind. That thought brought me even higher as Will gripped my auburn ponytail and steeled me for what turned out to be a wild ride. His rock-hard body slammed into mine with each thrust. The combination of the action and the thought of my man watching everything had me slippery wet, with juices dripping down my inner thighs.

"God, you're hot," Will sighed as he bucked against me.

"On fire—" I agreed, pushing back into him, meeting and matching him stride for stride. I didn't look up to the second floor as I came. I closed my eyes and let the world disappear. Will brought his fingertips to my swollen clit, extending the pleasure for me as he drove in deep.

"Where is he?" Will hissed against my neck. "Where?"

"Upstairs."

Will jutted his chin upward, and I felt a connection made between the three of us: me, Alden, and my new lover. Or should I say, "our" new lover?

"Tell him to come downstairs," Will demanded.

"You—" I told him, sighing. "Oh, Will, you do it."

He called out Alden's name, and then I heard the sound of feet on the steps, and the screen door opening. I looked up to see my man standing there, a waiting, willing smile on his face.

California dreaming? Maybe. But every once in a while even the most fantastic dreams can come true.

NAKED?
NEVER!

I'm not a fighter, but I am never without my protection.

I'm not a warrior, but I always wear armor. As strong as iron. As tough as steel. I can't imagine leaving my apartment without it. I'd feel exposed. People would see me, *really* see me, and I couldn't handle that. As long as I am suited up, I feel powerful and in control. Without my gear, I would be naked, and that's an impossibility for me. For years my personal motto has been simply this:

Naked? Never.

My first piece of armor was a battered leather jacket purchased for sixty dollars at a Soho thrift store. Huge, black, and ugly, the thing had an attitude all its own. The sleeves hung well past my fingertips, and the body of the coat fell practically to my knees. From the moment I first put my hands through the sleeves, I knew its power. My stride lengthened. My dark brown eyes took on a sharper glow. My posture was straighter. When

I wore that jacket, I felt strong. Immovable. It was my cloak of invisibility. I'd slip it on and disappear into its welcoming depths. I can still close my eyes and conjure up the smell of the old leather; remember the softness of the interior, cavelike and warm. That special coat kept me safe for years, and even after its function faded, I stored it in the back of my closet, where I could stroke the surface for strength whenever I needed an extra charge.

In college, I discovered that I didn't have to disappear in order for my protective shield to be working. "All black" served the purpose just fine—even formfitting, sexy black would work for me. In a sleek dress and killer high-heeled boots, I was unstoppable. In a velvet stretch-top covered with skulls, I exuded power. With my black hair, dark eyes, and pale skin, I could be goth without trying, dark without death. Nobody ever called me on my color choice. No one ever seemed to notice where my power came from. I reveled in my ability to get away with my secret—although I might appear waiflike and feminine, I was never without armor.

It took several years of dating before I was forced to explain my style to a lover. All New Yorkers own closets filled with black. I'd simply turned mine into a sense of self-preservation. In my suit of armor, I am steel coated. With dark ruby lipstick and an ice-cold stare, I am all powerful. And while Jonah admired my expensive collection of clothes, he wanted to go beyond them. He wanted to find out about the woman beneath.

He tried subtle ways at first, attempting to undress me for sex. But I was on to him, and I took the lead. I undressed myself, down to the basics, and then I went on my knees and undid his fly and sucked him down. He forgot his intentions, swallowed up by his lust. He allowed me to keep on my satin tap panties and demi bra, reveling in the sensation of my mouth on his cock.

Only afterward, collapsed on the sofa, did he remember how the evening had started.

"I wanted to strip you," he said, confused at the change of plans, but too sex-drunk to figure out how I'd taken over.

"I got to you first."

"But you never let me see you naked. You've got an amazing body. Why hide it?"

I touched myself through the sheer undies. "I'm not hiding anything."

"You are," he insisted. "You dress up for me. You wear any sort of costume I request. But you won't let me see you bare," Jonah said. "So how about naked?"

"Naked? Never." The words slipped out before I could stop myself.

"Never?"

"Okay, right," I conceded. "In the shower. In the tub. Occasionally, in a private sauna. But no other time."

"Not even alone? When you're in your apartment all by yourself? What about then?"

How to explain? I couldn't. I didn't have the words. All I knew was that naked was not safe. Jonah waited, quiet, patient. I gave him a quick headshake, feeling my curls fall free around my flushed cheeks. I let my eyes glance downward to see if I really did still have my clothes on, and then I sighed with relief. Why? Because naked equals exposed. And I'm never exposed.

"Naked?" he repeated.

"Never."

"Never?"

I like my armor. After six years, I'm used to it. I'm protected.

"Even with sex?"

Definitely with sex. *Of course*, with sex. Different armor is called for during romantic interludes, but armor, nonetheless. Lingerie armor. Black lace armor. The sort of sexy nothings that men—at least, the men I've been with up to Jonah—have never realized stood for anything at all. But for me, they're as serious as battlefield armor. Even a G-string offers protection. I've never been entirely nude with a man. No previous lover ever thought to complain.

"Take them off."

I looked at the camisole and tap panties. They were sheer black, edged in lace. To me, they were made of steel reinforcements.

"No," I said, "No. Never...."

"Never," Jonah repeated, and I could see that he was trying to recall our past encounters. The merry widow. The corset with stockings. The La Perla that cost a week's pay. The velvet-trimmed nightie. "Never," he repeated softly. "Okay, baby. That's gotta change."

My armor has protected me since I realized that I had a body. Since I decided to protect that body.

"Slowly," he said, but his tone was empathetic.

"Slowly," I repeated, looking into his bottle-green eyes. "So slowly." Thinking: *Naked.*

Never?

We started with a game. He'd take off one piece of clothing. Then I would. His jeans. My black jersey dress. His T-shirt. My stockings. He didn't push me. He fucked me while I still had on my lacy crotchless panties and iridescent noir push-up bra. He fucked me against the wall while he whispered to me, "I'm going to take off all your clothes. I'm going to strip you down and look at you, really look at you." I shuddered all over, and then I came. Harder than hard. Harder than ever.

The next time, we went a step further. "You undress me,"
he said. "You do all the work." I was on him immediately, and
I liked it. I unbuttoned his top, undid his fly with my teeth. I
spread the clothes around him on the bed and feasted on him.
I got to stay dressed, and that made me feel invincible. The
only thing I lost was my lipstick, spread around the base of his
cock and up and down the shaft. When we were finished, I was
mussed, but still protected. He was entirely naked, his body
decorated with the blood-red stains of my lipstick kisses.

The night after, we got closer to the truth. After an evening
spent at a dance club in the city, he stripped me. I felt my heart
pounding. Heard the blood rushing in my ears. But he took pity
once again. He got me down to my thong and bra set, then
flipped me over and fucked me doggie-style, plucking the floss of
the thong out of the way in order to gain entrance.

So maybe he did understand, I thought. Maybe he realized
that fucking with clothes on was okay. Or maybe he was willing to give me this little flaw, this little mental glitch. Could it
be that he'd leave it at the teasing? Telling me he would have
me bare, but letting me slip away with something to wear for
protection?

But no...

The next night, he requested a striptease. "It will be fun," he
assured me. "Sexy and sweet." I knew I could have layers, and
this eased my mind. I thought he would stop me before I got to
the base. I thought he understood the fear that coursed through
me. The music was undeniably cliché—silly even. But erotic
almost in spite of itself. A standard, a classic: "You Can Leave
Your Hat On."

"You can," Jonah said.

"Excuse me?"

"Leave your hat on."

"I'm not wearing a hat," I said, stating the obvious.

"You can *put* a hat on," he suggested, eyebrows raised.

I looked at his collection of vintage ball caps and then shook my head.

"Go on," he said. "Choose your armor."

"They don't offer much protection."

"You won't need any more. Trust me."

We stared at each other in silent battle. Then I shrugged and moved over to the wall. This was Jonah's game. I had to trust him or it wouldn't be worth playing at all. After a moment's consideration, I plucked a faded blue one from the rack and slid my ponytail through the back. "Now," he said, starting the music up again. "With each piece of clothing," he said, "tell why."

"Why?"

"Why you need any sort of armor in the first place."

"The looks," I explained as I peeled off my top.

"Looks?"

"From men."

"But it's me looking."

"I know."

"So what's the problem?"

I shrugged. I didn't really have a clue. All I knew was that naked was scary. Even with the little tender underthings, I could protect myself. But tonight was the night. Jonah wanted a complete reveal. As the music continued, I peeled off each item.

"Did someone ever say something nasty to you?"

"Nasty?"

"Mean—"

I shook my head. That wasn't it. This wasn't about being judged. I simply have always reveled in the safety of being undercover.

"But what about the boldness of showing yourself off? Can't you see the power in that?"

I moved my hips to the music, and I thought about what he was saying. I was down to my black velvet bra and panties—and that ball cap. I saw Jonah watching me, and then I saw past him, saw my reflection in the mirror. Cocking my head at myself, I flipped the straps down my arms, showing Jonah my breasts.

It's not that I've never had a man look at my breasts before, or touch them, or play with them, but I've always had something on—a bra to kiss through, a sheer camisole, a bikini top. At twenty-two, that shouldn't be entirely shocking. But Jonah seemed to think so. He sucked in his breath as I pulled off my bra, and I suddenly understood what he meant. I did feel power. I felt as powerful as when fully clothed.

"Please," Jonah said, reaching out for the waistband of my panties. "Please, baby—"

I grinned at him. This was a new feeling, this raw heat running through me. While gazing into his eyes, I slowly pulled my panties down my thighs and then let them drop to the floor. I was undressed, exposed, and radiant with desire. Jonah motioned for me to come to the bed. I took my time, still moving to the music. I knew that fucking this time would be different. I knew that fucking from now on would be different—that dressing would be different—that *everything* would be different.

Jonah gripped me around the waist and pulled me so that I was astride his naked body. I could look down at his handsome face, or look straight ahead at the reflection of my naked body. Both images were equally sexy. I slid my hips upward and then rocked down on Jonah's cock. He tilted his head back and groaned. I worked him harder, pumping my thighs up and down, riding him in a driven rhythm, back and forth. My clit gained contact with his flat stomach whenever I rocked my hips

forward, and I could tell that this was going to make me come.
This and the power of being naked.

Nobody ever told me about that. Nobody ever explained that while you can gain protection by being draped from head to toe, naked can be even more extreme.

I pushed myself up on Jonah's body, then slid back down. I arched my back and pushed my breasts out to him, and felt his hands come up to cup them. I shivered at the sensation of his fingertips on my naked breasts—naked, entirely naked—and then I sighed as he let one hand slip down lower, finding my clit, touching me there without any barrier. I sucked in my breath and slid up and down again, not shutting my eyes, not closing him out.

I could see the pile of my black clothing on his bedroom chair, and I thought how strange that puddle of blackness looked. What would I wear to get home? Not all that. Surely not. What would I wear from now on?

Jonah tapped at my clit, and I locked eyes with him and said, "I'm gonna—"

"I know."

"I'm gonna come—"

"You can leave your hat on," crooned Tom Jones, and I pulled that baseball cap off and tossed it to the floor.

My armor was inside. That's what I learned. I didn't need any battered jacket, any all-black wardrobe, any filmy nightie. I could be all powerful wearing nothing at all.

Not even a hat.

CHERRY
SLUSHEE

I don't know how I get myself into situations like this. None of my girlfriends ever seem to find themselves in such unusual positions. I guess I have a knack. A knack for getting myself into the stickiest sort of trouble. Of course, none of my girlfriends seem to have as much good sex as I do, so maybe the two go hand in hand—or hand in handcuff, or whatever.

Perhaps the real problem is just that I stay up way too late. When you're wide-eyed in the wee hours of the morning, your judgment can become impaired. Small circumstances take on large meaning. Everything depends on how the shadows play, on the shift and sway of car headlights dancing across a darkened wall.

The thing in this event was that I'd just gotten my own apartment, had only started to learn about living on my own. I thought there would be a huge enlightenment, or some sort of awakening that went with living solo. And there was. An awakening, anyway. The main change in my life was that I no longer slept regular hours. Being on my own meant I could stay up and paint all night if I wanted to, and that's what I ended up doing. Painting from ten at night until five in the morning, and then heading out to the local 24-hour grocery store to pick up breakfast foods and coffee. Often, I wouldn't crash until sometime late in the afternoon. I loved it. Despite the purple circles occasionally darkening the pale skin beneath my eyes. Despite the fact that I couldn't manage to do brunch with friends any longer and they started referring to me as "the vampire." To me, living alone equaled freedom, and freedom meant not living—or sleeping—by anyone else's schedule.

And that's how I got myself in such a sticky situation. By not sleeping. But sticky can be good. That's what my brunch-loving friends don't realize. Sticky can be sweet, much sweeter than being clean, and washed, and sliding in between the sheets at a quarter to eleven. Sticky can be much more exciting than having to wake up every morning at half-past six.

I was pretty sure I wasn't the only one who felt this way. There was a handsome checker at the grocery who seemed to like working odd hours. He watched me whenever I went running in for my post-midnight supplies, and we began a regular, flirtatious conversation, each part continuing the next night. We could have gone on indefinitely, I suppose, bantering before dawn until one of us got bold. Then one night he mentioned that he was going to be clocking out early, at three instead of five, and he wanted to know if I was free.

"At three?" I asked.

He gave me a smile, as if he understood what an odd sort of time it was for a date. "Working here can make it difficult to keep a regular social schedule," he confessed. "But you seem to like being up at night."

I nodded, feeling him looking me over. I was paint-stained, as always, and a bit disheveled, but he seemed to like what he saw. "Wanna get a drink?"

"Yeah," I said quickly. "Yeah."

The only thing open close by besides the grocery store was a convenience store on the corner, so after a brief discussion of our lack of options, we went there for Slushees. We sat outside, in the chill predawn air, and I shivered all over as I got that first thrilling headrush of cherry Slushee.

He watched me shudder with the chill, and he grinned and touched my arms. "You don't have to finish it," he said softly.

"I do."

"Why?"

"You bought it for me—"

"And what does that mean?"

"It makes it special."

I don't know why, but he understood that. This was our first date. Three A.M. Outside of a 7-Eleven, following none of the rules that my girlfriends live by. But I have my own set of rules, and I was going to drink that cherry Slushee until the ruby-dyed ice stained my lips dark pink. Until I was shivering all over, cold to the core. Until he put his strong arm around me, holding me tight to his body as I swallowed the last sweet drop. I rested my head on his shoulder, reveling in the warmth of him after devouring such a chilling treat.

"Where to?" he asked softly, speaking against my dark hair.

I knew right then that we were going to fuck. I knew when he bought me the Slushee. Jesus, I knew when he said, "Wanna get a drink?" Sometimes you know. We were only two blocks away from my place, and I laced my fingers with his, paying attention to how large his hand was. Sure, I know what people say—you can't tell anything from that. But they're wrong. Hand size might not be an indicator of cock size, but you *can* guess how a large hand might feel against your ass if it were delivering a few stinging strokes of a bare-bottomed spanking. You can gauge from the grip if a man is into control, or more likely to take a backseat role.

I could tell that he was in charge, even as he let me lead him to my place. I could tell from the way he circled my waist with his arm, from the way that he took my key out of my hands and opened the door for me. He stopped me in the entryway and kissed my sticky cherry lips and said, "I've been thinking about those lips of yours from the first time I saw you."

"Yeah," I teased, "what were you thinking?"

"About how sweet they'd feel around my cock." As he spoke, he pushed me down, his hands firm on my shoulders. I felt my knees bend, felt myself go into that automatic pre-cock-sucking position. I was excited, hungry, and curious—watching as he undid the fly of his jeans and let me see him for the first time. I had my face up close, breathing in to smell the faded fabric of his denim jeans, the warmth of his hidden skin. I wanted to suck. I was ready for him, drawing him into the chill of my mouth, still so cold from the Slushee, but he didn't care. He warmed me rather than letting me cool him down. He played me, his fingers slipping through my hair, his body pressing back and forth, rocking me, working with me while he spoke.

"God, I couldn't think when I saw you that first time. All covered in paint. So dirty, and you didn't care. You just went out like that."

My girlfriends are the type who polish up before exiting their apartments. Can't be seen without makeup, a blow-dry, an "outfit." I've known them all since high school, and we have history together. But we share nothing else.

"I liked that," he said. "I liked that you were mussed, but

still so pretty, and you didn't care that there was a blue streak of paint on your cheek, or that your jeans had holes."

He slid in and out of my mouth as he spoke, and I swallowed hard on him, rather than try to keep up my end of the conversation. I would have drained him right there, in the entry to my tiny apartment, if he'd let me. But as I'd gauged from the way his hand gripped mine, he was planning on being in charge. And his idea of the evening—excuse me, the *morning*—didn't end with a blow job by the front door. After letting me wet him with my mouth, he lifted me up, this time in his arms, and carried me down the short hallway to the bedroom.

This was where I painted. A large easel sat in the middle of the room, and my tiny bedroll lay sprawled against one wall. It actually showed how little I cared for the concept of sleep. Now, I wished I had a king-size, something luxurious and dreamy for him to toss me onto. He set me down gently, and then looked over my art supplies, his eyes finally settling on a roll of twine I used to tie paper to my finished canvases before transporting them for show.

With a length of twine, he tied me up—wrists together, ankles bound—and then gave me a kiss on the lips. "Be right back," he murmured.

I didn't ask. I just nodded. In five minutes, he'd returned, with another Slushee. I trembled all over when I saw it, not sure how I knew what to expect, but expecting just the same. I knew he didn't plan on having me drink that, and I knew he wasn't going to sit at my side and slurp up the crushed ice himself. I was right.

While I watched, he drew the Slushee in with the straw and used the flavored ice to decorate my skin—my nipples, my collarbone, a lone line down the basin of my belly.

"Oh, god—" I moaned.

He followed each magic line of the straw with the warmth of his mouth.

"Oh, yes—" I said next.

To my utter delight, he took turns, first drawing designs on my naked skin with the iced cherry confection and then retracing those same patterns with his tongue. I thrashed on the bedroll, made crazy by the combination of the cold and the heat, by the tempting slow way that he worked me. I couldn't decide what it was that I wanted—or more truly, I couldn't fathom that I really wanted what I thought I did. Which was this: the Slushee, that cold, chilling Slushee, right on my clit. Oh, yes, that's what I wanted. Even as I shivered all over, trembling with all my might, I desperately wanted him to lift the straw and streak a line of deep fuchsia iced Slushee over my clit.

"Do it," I told him. "Oh, please."

"You really want me to." It wasn't a question. He knew me that well already. It wasn't a question at all. But I answered, despite the lack of querying tone in his voice. I locked my eyes on his, and I licked my bottom lip, and I said. "Yes. Go on. Go on and do it."

I watched him suck a bit of the melting drink up the straw, capture the liquid with his thumb over the tip, and then bring the straw right over my pussy. I thought of how people play with candle wax, straining against the heat, and I wondered which sensation was more pleasurable. I thought of those silly conversations you have when you're a kid, teasing your friends with horror tales: How would you rather die? In fire or in ice? I had time to think those thoughts before he lifted his thumb and released the river of slushed cherry ice over my desperately waiting clit, and then I lifted my hips off the thin makeshift mattress and screamed. The sensation was overpowering. So cold. So fucking cold. Everything in my body tensed, as if my muscles had gotten some message to lock down. Before I could make any noise again, begging, howling, whimpering, crying, he settled himself between my legs and brought his mouth to my pussy and began to lick. Hot against my cold, drinking my juices mixed and mingled with the melted Slushee.

As soon as I relaxed into the warmth of his mouth, he reached for the Slushee again. I didn't say no. I didn't say yes. I just closed my eyes and held my breath and waited. Again, the coldest river of juices poured over me, and then his mouth followed immediately, warming where the ice had kissed my naked skin. Over and over he dripped and drank until I came, in a cherry-wave of pleasure, bucking and pulling on the twine, knowing I'd have marks on my skin, and not caring one bit. The climax rocked me, and I didn't have the ability to see what was going to happen next, didn't guess that as soon as I came, he'd have another plan.

He did.

He was moving as I came. Instead of using a straw, he scooped iced Slushee with his fingers and spread a finger full into the mouth of my pussy. I groaned so loud, my eyes open now, watching as he shifted so that his cock could dive inside of me where the ice and heat were waiting.

Now, he fucked me. Fucked me with an intensity I couldn't believe. Not only the cherry Slushee melted, but I felt as if I had melted into him. My body, my fears, my desires. I melted into a pool of sticky syrup, a puddle of Slushee from a 24-hour market. Who'd ever have guessed that ninety-nine cents could bring a girl that much pleasure?

We ruined the white twin sheets with the staining cherry dye. But I tingle all over when I think back on that night. My girlfriends don't understand when I try to explain these sorts of situations. How I get myself in such sultry messes. What *they'd* consider messes. What I consider sticky-sweet. Because now I don't have any incentive to return to a normal schedule, to sleep from eleven to seven and go about the day like the rest of the world. I like the midnight hours. I like going to the 24-hour grocery right before he punches out, and then walking hand in hand to the 7-Eleven for our standard, icy dessert.

None of my friends seem to get the appeal. Maybe I'm crazy. Or maybe I just need a new set of girlfriends. But before that, I need another cherry Slushee.

MEN AT WORK

Maybe there's no such thing as love at first sight, but lust at first sight...well, that's a different story altogether. Because that's what I had, and I had it bad. Lust for the dark-haired, dark-eyed captain of a rough and rowdy road crew.

The crew had been out in our little rural community for weeks. Trimming trees. Moving boulders. And making me want to come. Not all of them. Just one of them. A fiercely handsome man with a sleek mustache and sparkling brown eyes. He'd look at me when he was the one holding up the stop sign, and I'd look back through the windshield, flush, and look away. How many times? Three, four, every fucking time I went to do an errand. And I went to do more errands than usual when I knew they were at work. I put on elaborate makeup just to go to the grocery store. Normally a jeans and T-shirt type of girl, I wore skirts and high-heeled leather boots and I took extra time styling my long black hair.

After several weeks of visual foreplay, I got bold. I held his eye contact and stared back at him, gazed through my cherry-flush, forcing the connection. He liked that. He tilted his head at me and narrowed his eyes, and I could almost hear what he was thinking: *Take me on? Is that what you think you're doing, little girl? You think you can take me?*

The men were connected to one another with walkie-talkies, letting each other know when cars were waiting at either side of the roadwork. One afternoon, I watched a heavyset man radio another while the stop sign was in place. After a moment, he flipped the sign to *slow,* and motioned me forward. As I drove around the winding roads, I spotted a golden-yellow work truck in my rearview mirror. Was it him? How was I supposed to find out?

I kept on my normal route and saw the truck holding steady, so I finally pulled into the dirt lot of a local park. Empty. Totally empty. Surrounded by trees. Hidden. The truck pulled in behind me, and my man got out. I knew in my head what I wanted to do, but I didn't know whether people really behaved like that outside of porno movies. Could I step from my convertible, rush over, and tell him what to do to me? Turned out I didn't have to. He knew. True doms can always sniff out a sub.

With a nod of his head, he motioned for me to come toward him. I slid from my seat, slammed the door behind me, and walked to the back of his truck. As soon as I was in his range, he gripped onto my shoulders and brought me into his arms for a kiss—the kiss I'd imagined since I first saw him. Hot and fast, his mouth firm against mine, his teeth finding my bottom lip and then biting it hard. Then, because it had to happen, because it was right, he pushed me down on the gravel-strewn dirt and unbuttoned his deeply faded jeans. I was ready, my lips parted, mouth open, but he stopped me before I could act. Quickly, he pulled his heavy leather belt free from his jeans, and with me in the exact position he wanted, he captured my wrists tightly behind my back.

"Such a tease," he said, running his fingers roughly under my chin, tilting my head upward with a jerk. "Such a fucking tease."

I sighed, so hungry now, so desperate, but he wasn't ready to give in. All I wanted was the taste of his cock in my mouth, and I wanted it more than anything I've ever craved, yet he wouldn't let me suckle from him. With one hand still under my chin, he ran the back of his free hand against my cheek, softly, making me tremble all over at the gentleness of his touch. Then his hand came up high in the air, and he slapped my cheek, catching me off guard, making me bite down on a moan. I lowered my head, shuddering all over, feeling how wet my panties were growing. Feeling how much I needed this. Needed him to treat me exactly the way he was.

"Look at me, baby," he insisted, and I raised my head.

Now he pushed forward, butting against my lips with the head of his cock. Oh, god; oh, Christ, was I ready. I wanted to drink, wanted to drain, wanted to swallow him whole. But still he wouldn't let me. He plunged in, taking his pleasure, then slid back out and bent to rub my nipples forcefully through my thin white blouse. He pinched them hard, and I arched and groaned, and while my mouth was open, he slid his cock in again. Each time he played me, he made me wetter still. So that I didn't know what I was doing anymore. All I knew was I had the need—the urgency—to drink him down.

"Bad girl," he said, "lost in your little games. Cruising the curves in your silver convertible. And all you want is for some-one to fuck that sweet mouth of yours. Isn't that right?"

I think I nodded. I know I moaned. And he let me, finally,

let me have at him. I swallowed with a vengeance. I sucked and
pulled, my cheeks indenting with the intensity of my hunger. He
held me steady with his rough hands on my shoulders, pinned
me in place in his strong grip. My eyes wide open, I saw the trees
behind him, saw his scuffed work boots below, the dirt under
my knees. It was a relief to be allowed to use my mouth, to trick
my tongue up and down his straining rod. I almost cried with
the release of tasting the first drops of his precum.

When I could think of nothing more than draining his every
drop, he pulled out again, lifted me up by my arms, and bent me
over. Holding me steady, my skirt captured up at my waist, he
slid my panties all the way down my legs and waited for me to
step out of them. Then he punished my naked ass with his large
open hand, spanking me hard and fast. All my faith was in him.
He had the total control to keep me balanced, so that I wouldn't
fall forward against the gravel, so that I wouldn't collapse on
the ground. I had no thoughts now; I simply let him take me.
Let him push me back down again onto the scraped raw skin of
my knees, so that I could open my mouth wide and suck him.
Sweetly suck him. My mouth earning the pleasure of the power
he imparted.

Up and down my tongue tricked against his shaft. In and
out his cock plunged, searching out the warm wet heat of my
throat. I was delirious with the pleasure of serving him. Breathing deeply, I memorized his smell, the way his skin felt against
my cheeks, the way my ass smarted under the gauzy fabric of my
summer-weight skirt. Then he was once again in motion, lifting me up and bringing me to the back of the truck. My wrists
were still bound behind my back, so he had to slide my skirt up
for me, kicking my legs wider apart, pushing into me with the
spit-slicked length of his erection. He fucked me so hard that his
truck shook. My face pressed into the metal of the truck bed; my

honeyed juices spilled down my thighs. And when we were finished, he simply unbuckled the well-worn belt and set me free.

But I didn't want to be free.

"You're calmer now, aren't you, girl?"

I thought about the words before I answered, and then I
nodded. He was right. All the nervous energy that had pulsed
through me each time we'd made eye contact was now gone.
I felt warm and in control. Better yet, I felt satisfied. I watched
him get into the truck and drive out of the lot. And although I
don't know when the road crew will be back, I do know that
I'll be ready.

HEAT

This is what she said: "I'd appreciate it if you didn't wear diaphanous clothing around my husband." And yes, I heard her. And yes, I understood both the cool, clear message and the icy tone of her voice. But the thing is, it was hot. Not just the weather—104 degrees in the shade, if you can believe it—but the way he looked at me. Let me tell you, it was so fucking hot, I almost melted under the intensity of his gaze.

He wanted me, and I wanted him, and it was summer. You know all about summer, right? Summer lovers, having a blast. Summer romance. Summer, summer, summer. Besides that, I was nineteen. What do you know about when you're nineteen? Nothing but the heat.

They had a giant lagoon-style pool, and whisper-quiet air-conditioning, and chilled Evian in the fridge, which I was supposed to pour into tall glasses over shaved ice (made of Evian as well), and serve with a twist of lemon in the morning and a twist of lime in the evening. They had a Spanish-style mansion high up in the hills, and drivers, and help—not just me, but a whole swarm of help. A lady who did their laundry. A man who detailed their cars. A cook for day and a cook for night.

I had a beat-up hand-me-down car that functioned mostly on my ability to pray really hard. I had a plug-in fan that did nothing but stir the heat around my Hollywood apartment. I had diaphanous clothing, which I wore to my best advantage, and had been wearing long before I landed the job as personal assistant to the actress and her director husband.

What I didn't have was an agenda. I wasn't that smooth yet. But I was hot.

Physically. Mentally. Diaphanously.

I didn't wear the sundress to annoy the wife. I wore it because it was 104 degrees in the shade and the only thing less constricting to wear would have been nothing. This is what I said in my defense. But I didn't say it to her; I said it to him when he walked into the kitchen to remind me about the Evian over Evian rule. *Evian* ice. I'd never even considered making ice cubes from bottled water—but then, I never bought bottled water even for drinking. The expense was too much for my minuscule budget, while water from the faucet was free. Yet here, in the Hollywood Hills, the actress sprayed her face with Evian. She washed her hair with it. She had a fixation on twists. Lime for morning. Lemon for night. No, wait! It was the other way around. I had to check my notes. I'd only been a personal assistant for a week.

"Lime," the husband said kindly, his warm dark-brown eyes on mine. "Lime in the evening, and the sun is already setting."

I sighed and did my best to fish the curl of lemon out of the glass using one of their oddly shaped artistic forks.

"She'll taste the flavor in the water," he said. "She'll know there was lemon in it first. You'll have to start again."

"But what should I do with this?" I asked, holding up the glass. I couldn't imagine pouring bottled water down the drain.

"What do you *want* to do with it?"

His words made me smile, and I felt again how diaphanous my dress was. God, I liked that word, liked the way she'd used it in the sentence. "In the future, please do not wear diaphanous clothing around my husband." As if the husband had no control over himself whatsoever. As if the sight of me in a slinky dress would drive him directly out of her world and into my arms. As if *diaphanous* were a four-letter word.

Yes, the dress was sheer, but I had a slip on underneath. Yes, the slip was exactly the same color as my skin, and that's what made the dress seem so racy, but you could see much worse if you went down their twisting roads and into the sweltering heat of Hollywood. You could see tube tops and short shorts and acres of naked skin.

But there was more to her snide remark than the fact that my dress was thin and sexy. Her air-conditioning had raised my nipples, tenting the gauzy fabric. The heat of the day had given my skin a permanent flush not available at any cosmetic counter. Everything about the wife was cool and hard. Everything about me was hot and ready.

"So?" the husband asked.

"Truth?" I asked.

He leaned against the steel fridge and waited.

"I'd like to pour it over me." I paused, shocked myself at what I'd said. To counter the image, I added, "But that's such a waste." Then I bit my lip, because the woman, after all, *bathed* in the stuff.

He seemed to read my thoughts, because he laughed softly and said, "Does seem like a waste, doesn't it? But when you have *everything* then you have to work to create your luxuries.

Making your chef purchase caseloads of Evian for drinking and Evian for bathing is just such a luxury."

I looked around then, wondering why he felt so free to talk when his wife was somewhere in the house. Somewhere waiting for her water. He shrugged. "She's on the veranda, getting a pedicure." While he spoke, he came closer until he was standing right next to me. That smile still on his face, he gently took the glass from my hand. I knew what was going to happen a second before it did. He slowly tilted the glass so that the water ran over my collarbone and down the front of my dress, drenching me and making the sheer fabric completely translucent—or is that just another way to say "diaphanous"?

I didn't stop him. There was the heat, you know. And the fact that I was nineteen. And the fact that I knew I wouldn't be coming back again. Not after the comment about my clothing. And there was the air-conditioning blowing a satisfying chill through me, and the way his hands fit around my waist, and the whisper of his lips on my neck as he said, "You live in Hollywood, don't you?"

And I saw us together, him at my place in the old fifties building with the wrought iron railing and five flights of stairs. With the crown molding and the tap water and the endless inescapable heat. He poured a fresh glass of Evian and he motioned for me to tilt my head back. I closed my eyes as he let the water fall over my hair and my face, and I felt my own wetness meeting the wetness of the bottled water. Which was more pure? Which was more of a luxury?

Without bothering to refill the glass, he reached for the bottle, and poured the remaining contents all over me, showering me in front and behind with the precious water. I sighed and shivered, knowing that this was all inevitable: fucking up the water order, making out with the husband, losing my job.

He kissed me right there in the kitchen, kissed me dangerously, letting me stand there in my wet clothes, in the center
of a puddle on the expensively tiled floor. He was rough with
me through the transparent fabric of my dress, his hands doing
all those magical things that older lovers always seem to know
how to do—pinching my nipples, squeezing my waist, slapping
my ass so that the sound made a wet clapping echo in the large
room. He kissed me even harder, and then bit my bottom lip
and I sighed and squirmed at the sudden spark of pain. I knew
just what it would be like when we fucked, and I knew we
weren't going to fuck here. Not in the kitchen. Not so close to
the Evian.

"Leave me your address for your final paycheck," he said.

I gazed at him, waiting for an explanation.

"I'm sorry, but you have to understand that we just couldn't
possibly keep someone on staff who can't tell the difference between lime and lemon."

I smiled and nodded, then wrote my address down for him
on a pad by the phone. Slowly, as if moving through water, I got
my purse, stepping over the puddle on the floor, still feeling the
slick wetness of his lips on mine.

I headed outside to my old car, knowing that he'd come to
visit me that night, knowing that diaphanous had nothing to do
with it. Knowing that the actress could cool her house and chill
her Evian, but she couldn't stop the heat.

ALL
MCQUEEN'S
MEN

In the case of Julissa McQueen, it wasn't Humpty Dumpty
but a relationship that couldn't be put back together. Perhaps
it wasn't much of a relationship to start with, but Julissa had
tried for so long to put up with Raymond's innumerable idio-
syncrasies that she wasn't ready to give up on couplehood. Not
without a fight.

Turned out to be a big fight—a mean one, with Raymond
cruelly claiming that she'd obviously been unfaithful to him,
and Julissa storming out of the couple's penthouse apartment
in tears.

"You with your goddamn poker face," he called down the
hallway after her. "Finally, showing a little human emotion!
Didn't know you had it in you—"

Cliché, she thought as she stalked around the block, the
heels of her glossy knee-high black boots click-clacking on the
pavement. *Such a fucking cliché.* He couldn't accept her fiery

independence, so he chose to attack her rather than deal with his own insecurities. The thing of it was that she *hadn't* ever cheated. Not on Raymond nor any one of her previous boyfriends. The concept didn't fit her style. If a connection with a man faded, she ended the relationship before moving on to the next one.

Sure, she might have had a *thought* of cheating—but who didn't? Once or twice when an interesting specimen looked her way, she lost herself in a decadent daydream involving a satisfying situation with someone new. Perhaps while on the subway, or at the grocery store, or out on a morning run. But she'd never actually gone through with it.

Now that Raymond claimed she had—and she was fuming at the false accusation—she thought that maybe she should. Why be blamed for something, be punished for it, really, without experiencing the pleasure of actually screwing someone else?

Someone else named Blake.

And someone else named Sam.

And even someone else named Nelson.

Yes, she had them all lined up in her mind, and as she turned the corner and entered her favorite English bar, All The King's Horses, there they were, as if they'd been magically positioned, waiting for her: All McQueen's Men.

In truth, they were her poker buddies. She loved the game, had been a pro for years, but she'd never had much luck playing cards with girls. Ladies didn't seem to put as much thought into the mental war play of poker. Generally speaking, girls lost interest in their hands and started talking about clothes, or hair, or men. Julissa couldn't stand that. When *she* played cards, she wanted serious adversaries, men who had no qualms about taking her money. She wanted poker faces.

Raymond wasn't into cards. He liked playing the ponies. Or

watching football on television. He didn't understand why she felt the need to join her buddies in the smoke-filled private room at the bar, where Nelson, who owned the place, had a weekly game. Raymond was invited, but after going twice, he backed out permanently. Julissa came every week. Or rather, attended every week. Mentally, she came every once in a while when thinking about what might take place with the three studly guys who joined her at the green felt-flocked table.

Tonight was the night she'd find out.

"There she is," Blake grinned at her, motioning to the others that she'd arrived. "Let the games begin."

Julissa just smiled as she brushed a lock of midnight hair out of her startling cat-shaped eyes, and then followed the trio to the back room. Before anyone could cut the deck of cards this evening, Julissa perched herself on the edge of the table and said, "Let's raise the stakes tonight—"

Sam tilted his head at her as he waited for her to continue.

"What's on your mind?" Nelson wanted to know.

"Strip poker," Blake guessed, patting Julissa on the back with one of his large hands, touching her in an almost buddy-style that lingered just a beat too long for someone who wanted to be strictly friends.

"No," she said, shaking her head. Her long, dark hair tickled against her cheeks. "Fuck poker."

"Fuck *poker*?" Sam repeated, shocked. "What do you mean? You don't like playing with us anymore?"

"She's leaving us, boys," Blake said sadly, as if he'd always expected the day would eventually come, but had hoped against hope that it wouldn't arrive so soon.

"Not 'fuck the game,'" she quickly explained, reaching for the deck of cards and shuffling expertly. The cards danced mesmerizingly between her fingers. "But a game played for the stakes of fucking—" Another hesitation. "Fucking me, that is." One final pause. "If you're interested."

She watched the men carefully to see when they would get it. One by one, she saw the moments when they understood what she was saying—and one by one, they nodded in agreement, nodded as if they didn't care if she were pulling their chains, they definitely wanted in. Julissa herself wasn't entirely sure of what she was saying. She knew what she needed. Had thought about it enough, honestly, to have the scene entirely choreographed from start to finish. Handsome Sam would be in front of her, his faded blue jeans open, cock out, and she would lick from his balls to the tip of his shaft as Blake slid her soft skirt up to her hips and lowered her panties. Tonight, she had on a pair of pale lilac-colored ones made of lace-trimmed silk.

She wanted Nelson between her legs, fiercely lapping her pussy while Blake prepared her to receive his cock from behind, backdoor style. And by backdoor, she really meant that she wanted Blake to take her ass. Raymond wouldn't do that with her. Not that he hadn't ass-fucked a girl before, because he had and she knew it. They'd teased each other with one of those "what have you done" conversations early on in their relationship, in the playful stage before they'd gotten serious. So yeah, she knew he'd done it anally with a French girl in New York one summer. But he didn't do it that way with Julissa, and for some reason his refusing only made her want to go that route even more.

So she saw it all, had fantasized about it so often she felt as if she'd seen the image in a dirty movie, but that didn't mean it was going to happen. The boys had to win first, and winning wouldn't be easy. Julissa was an ace at poker. Nobody ever knew exactly what she was thinking.

"Really?" Sam asked now, and Julissa realized that her poker face was already in place. The guys truly didn't know whether or not she was putting them on.

"Really," Julissa said, dealing out the first hand.

"And Raymond?" Blake asked.

"Fuck Raymond," Julissa spat. It was clear to all of them that "fuck Raymond" was an entirely different statement from "fuck poker," and none of the men commented further. They sat down, eyeing each other carefully, and lifted their cards.

Even though she wanted this fantasy to come true more than anything else she'd ever wanted, Julissa couldn't lose on purpose. That wouldn't be right. But the guys turned out to want the evening's culmination even more than she did. For the first time ever, they created a three-man team, and they fought hard, all of them, to beat her down. Which they did. As soon as she started to lose, Julissa felt that the inevitable was happening. She couldn't draw the cards she needed, couldn't fake the boys out with any of her standard moves. Slowly, she began to accept that her fantasy was going to come true, and that made the cards shake in her hands.

"Nervous?" Sam asked, reaching out to stroke her knee gently under the table.

"No," she said, folding her final hand, and she realized as she said the word that she wasn't nervous at all. She was excited, desperately wet, and ready to get started. "Let me tell you how it's going to be—"

They listened carefully to her precise instructions, and then they took their positions around her. Sam was in front, as he had to be, with his jeans splayed open, awaiting the first gentle lick of her tongue on his naked cock. He looked down at her in total awe, as she parted her full berry-glossed lips and let him in. And just as she surrounded Sam's cock with her open mouth, Nelson lowered her panties and pressed his face against her pussy.

"Oh—" Julissa murmured, her mouth full of Sam. "Oh, yes."

Blake didn't jump in right away. He watched the action for several moments before wetting his fingers and tracing them around Julissa's rear hole. He wanted her nice and wet before he plunged, and he wanted a signal from her that this was really what she needed.

Nelson continued to suckle on her clit, and Julissa, bent forward, had her mouth so full of Sam's cock that she couldn't talk at all. But she waggled her lovely ass a little, left and then right, to let Blake know that she was ready. He parted her cheeks wider and then pressed the head of his cock at her asshole. He waited a moment, and then slid in a little bit deeper. Julissa moaned ferociously around Sam's cock, and Sam picked up the pace, sliding back and forth between her lips at a rapid rhythm. Julissa couldn't get enough of him. She swallowed forcefully, and then reached forward to cradle his balls as she continued to work him. She was driven on by the pace of Nelson between her legs and Blake fucking her smoothly from behind. Being taken back there was as exciting as she'd dreamed of. The fact that Raymond had been denying it to her so long made the pleasure even greater.

The foursome were so self-contained that not one of them heard the knock on the private door, and none noticed the intrusion until they heard a sharp intake of breath, followed by, "What the fuck is going on back here!"

Then Blake looked over his shoulder, raised his eyebrows, and simply shrugged. He was too close to coming to stop at this point. Sam didn't even bother with that much of a response, paying attention instead to the lovely Julissa, gently cradling her head as she sucked him to the root, swallowing every last drop. From his position, Nelson couldn't really see Raymond very clearly, but he knew the man was there. Being watched had always thrilled Nelson, and he put one hand on his own bulging crotch as he continued to lick Julissa's pulsing clit. He was going to come at the moment she did, and that made his entire body feel alive with impending ecstasy.

As for Julissa, when she glanced over at Raymond's face, she felt a wave of satisfaction beat through her—in the back room of All The King's Horses, and in the midst of All McQueen's Men, it was obvious that this was one relationship that would never be put back together again.

But some stories are like that—for Julissa, it didn't make her evening's ending any less happy.

BLADES

It's hard to steal a knife. More difficult, say, than palming an apple, the rounded red fruit cupped under your hand in an arc as you slide between the automatic glass doors of the neighborhood grocery. Far more complicated than lifting a lipstick. Those short, cylindrical tubes always fit so easily beneath the edge of a cuff before disappearing up the sleeve in a reverse magic trick. Trust me, knives take skill. And more than that, they take will. You have to want to steal that shiny, mirrored blade, to conceal it carefully, so that you don't cut yourself to bits in the process.

The cutting, of course, comes later.

That said, I'm the type of girl who gets an intense rush from any type of thievery. From absconding successfully with a single piece of fruit that I know I'll never eat to taking lipsticks and glosses and tints that simply gather dust on my bathroom shelf. The art of stealing is enough. It transforms me. A heart-pounding energy fills my brain when I realize that, fuck yes, I'm going to do it once again. I'm going to walk out of this store with something that I haven't paid for. Fear freezes into a pleasing numbness as I grip an item tightly and make my way to the nearest exit.

But knives are the best, because blades turn me on.

I've been at the game for a number of years. I know what I'm doing. You'd never guess my sexual hobby from looking at me. I've mastered the nonchalant expression that I wear as I cruise the cutlery section of a gourmet cooking store. I'm no cat burglar. You won't find me robbing a place after hours, scuttling through deserted racks of silverware accompanied only by my shadow and the red light on the video camera overhead. What's the fun in that? I like the challenge of working when people are present. Security guards. Overly attentive shopgirls. And other customers. *Especially* other customers. Those housewives who trundle along after a new paring knife, one with a handle that won't break off this time, thank you very much. The atrocious newlyweds exchanging a set of butter knives for a fancy blade that will cut through the slimy seaweed skin of homemade sushi.

"We're making it ourselves," they gush in saccharine-sweet voices, eyes on each other rather than the prices of the expensive weapons displayed before them.

But my eyes are focused on the razor-sharp edges that can do such damage in the hands of those less experienced, and even more damage in the hands of those who know what they're doing. I like the high-end knives, often imported from Europe, with black handles made of heavy-duty rubber. Usually, these blades are trapped behind glass. You have to ask for permission to touch.

"That one," I nod to the helpful, pink-cheeked salesgirl. "The small one."

I get wet as soon as the slick rubber meets the flesh of my

palm. My thumb works up the edge slowly, to dance lightly over
the ridge of the blade. It's a tango between steel and flesh, and
flesh, I know, will always lose. In my head, I can already visual-
ize the heartbreakingly lovely hue of that first drop of blood.
Cherry red, the little pinprick of liquid will dot and then swell,
blooming—

"Oh, gosh, Miss," the honey-blonde salesgirl murmurs.
"You've cut yourself."

And I have, which is shocking, to me as much as to her. I've
never done something like this before. Never let myself slip up
so badly in public. She is rightly concerned, taking me firmly by
the wrist, hurrying the two of us to a back room, where I see
a half-filled coffeemaker, a box of donuts that grow staler as I
watch. My dark brown eyes are clear and sharp. Everything is in
perfect focus. That line of blood as it trickles now, pooling—

"Raise up your arm," she says, lifting my hand to show me
what she wants me to do as she rummages through a cabinet
in search of bandages. The knife, I discover, is still in my other
hand, and I slide it secretly into my pocket without thinking.
Blade first. Down my thigh. If I sit, I'll stab myself.

"Here we go." Her voice is calm, and I recognize in it the
exact same tone that the nurse at my pediatrician's office always
used before bringing out a shot. "It'll sting," she warns, "but
only for a moment."

Rubbing alcohol is poured in a clear river on a puffball of
cotton. I don't feel the pain as the girl swipes the damp fluff
across my thumb. My head tilts back and I look at her. Soft
golden hair, a wisp over her forehead that she blows out of the
way with an exasperated breath. Flushed cheeks, dark gray eyes,
lips colored as red as that first drop of blood against my pale
skin. She notices me watching, but says nothing, applying pressure, careful and steady. I'm sure that she'll take out a Band-Aid

next, warn me about my carelessness before ushering me back into the real world of the busy store.

"What did you take the last time?" she asks, surprising me so greatly that I take a step back from her. I don't get far because she hasn't let go of my wrist. She's holding tight, and her eyes, not just gray now but the flat color of wet pavement, are gazing fiercely into my own. "It was a display knife, I think," she says, nodding in agreement with her own statement. "Am I right?"

Her fingers grip tightly into my wrist, holding onto my pulse point. I can feel my heart pounding where skin meets skin. There's the sound of a fire burning in my head. Rustling. White noise. I'm so confused that I can't speak.

"A Classe, from Italy," she says next, and the name is like a dirty word to me. Something hot and exciting. *Talk to me about knives,* I want to whisper to her. *Describe the rough edges of a serrated blade. The sleek lines of a parer. Whisper longingly to me about my favorites: the little ones, sharp and dangerous, like the dagger in my pocket.*

"I saw you," she says now. "And I waited for you to come back. I knew you couldn't stay away."

She'll turn me in, I think, picturing my first arrest ever. I see myself taken somewhere stark and frightening where I'll have to confess. I stole an apple, I remember. That was my first time. Lifted the sweet, ripe fruit from the pyramid of Washington red globes and got away before anyone could see. I took a lipstick next, I imagine myself saying—the words will pour from my lips in a rush. No one will be able to stop me. I took a lipstick, and then I wrote twisted things on my bathroom mirror. Perverted fantasies that looked as if they were etched on that frozen glass in blood.

"The back way," she says. "Follow me."

I move without thinking, having to do as she says since she

still hasn't released me from her powerful grip. As we hurry down the metal stairs of an employee exit, I notice the fresh scent of her shampoo, the sweet smell of her skin. Then we are suddenly in bright sunlight, walking out of the mall and to the parking lot. She takes me to a pickup truck, shiny and black, and soon we're inside together, on the leather seats. I squirm slightly, so as not to sever anything serious with my hidden prize. Simply knowing the knife is still in my pocket gives me strength.

Speaking in a voice that sounds nothing like my own, I hear myself giving directions to my apartment. I understand that when we get there, she'll see my loot: the blades in a row on a metal board, all of them pinned up there like prized butterflies in a lepidopterist's collection. This vision turns me on more than I can describe.

In silence, we drive the short distance to my place, and once she parks the truck, we move quickly from the empty street to the stark stone stairs to the bare patch of concrete outside my front door. My hands shake as I fumble with the key, until finally I make it work in the lock, and then we're inside in my spartan living room staring at each other. Without a word, she reaches into my pocket and comes up with the stolen goods. I sigh as I see her fingers close around the handle. It's like watching a porno movie, something sexual and tangible, raw and rough. And then she's turning me, slicing easily through the thin fabric of my long-sleeved black T-shirt. Tracing the very tip of the blade against my naked skin. Not cutting. Just letting me know how it's going to feel.

And it's going to feel like this—

Magically, the light grows brighter. Objects so often fuzzy in my vision take on clean edges. The knife presses harder and I hear my skin humming with the precursor to true pain, the only thing that clarifies my life and makes me come. She's talking now. I hear bits of sentences. While my vision is brighter, my hearing is focused only on the sound that a blade makes when it kisses skin. But I get snippets, and I make out certain key words: *Waited. Searched. Needed.* She needed to meet me as desperately as I needed to get caught.

There is artistry to what she's doing. Teasing me with that sharp, true point of my favorite sex toy: a knife. I'm contained in my black jeans, black boots, shreds of fabric that once made up my shirt. My long, gleaming dark hair is in a high ponytail off my neck. I can feel her breath on my skin, and I sense the moment before she presses harder. Before she brings the pain in home where I will really be able to feel it. I hold myself steady, feeling the wetness seep from between my nether lips, and I realize that stealing is nothing compared to this. The rush of taking something pales against the experience of being caught. And being punished.

The blade connects. My eyes close. My chin lifts.

With each flinty metal bite against my skin, my cunt contracts firmly. It pulses with a strong, regular rhythm, beats as if it has a heart of its own. In a flash, I know that if she works me long enough, hard enough, I will need nothing else. Pain enhances pleasure in the wet heat between my thighs. There is a perfect bliss each time she touches unmarked flesh. Every stolen item I've ever hidden away in my clothes has been practice for this.

She says, "Strip for me now. I want you naked."

As she steps back to give me room, I peel off my jeans for her, feeling my hand trembling at the button fly. Where is my calmness? Shivers ripple through me, but I manage to obey her command. In seconds, I'm nude, my clothes a discarded pile on the floor. Then I wait. She walks around me, observing in silence, and finally she comes forward and kisses me on the lips. Once. Again, I smell the different fragrances of her body that combine into one sweet scent. Breathtaking, almost overpowering. I close my eyes, drinking her in. With a single gesture, she demonstrates for me that she knows everything I want. Holding the blade in her hand, she gently rests the flat edge of it against my cheek, letting me feel the cold steel on my hot skin. I concentrate on that feeling, learning it, memorizing it.

Bending in front of me on her knees, she uses her free hand to part my pussy lips and she presses her mouth to my cunt, tasting me almost casually with a probing thrust of her tongue. A lick. A flicker of her wetness against my wetness. She's searching, quickly finding out how excited I am already, in the short space of time, from the teasing lines alone of the blade on my back.

The knife is still in her hand, and as she presses her lips against my waiting cunt, she starts to trace again, to sketch designs with the point of it. To illustrate for me how well she knows her craft. A blade pressed firmly into skin will leave a white mark, a momentary etching that lasts for several fleeting seconds without breaking the skin. Try it yourself. Drag one nail against the back of your hand and see how pretty the lines can look. They quickly fade. Too quickly. To make them last, you have to use something else. Something serious.

I look down and see her working the knife along my inner thighs, taking her time. She will mark me all over, I think. She will plan and diagram and then make the first cut. Can I wait? That's the question. The only question.

In the full-length windows across the room, I see the mirrored reflection of the two of us. I am naked; she is clothed. Her blonde hair is still in her face, effectively pushed out of her eyes every second or two with a practiced puff of her breath. My sleek, slim body appears so well-contained in comparison. Everything about me—my pale skin, dark hair, deep black eyes—radiates an inner cool, a quiet steadiness. Cutting through that surface shell will finally release me.

She works me steadily, alternating between the teasing lines of the blade against my flesh and scarlet-smeared kisses with her parted mouth. The sensations match each other in their ability to thrill me. Her wet, warm tongue trips between my parted pussy lips, spreading me open, pushing me wide. Her tongue makes circles, then diamonds, up and over my clit. A whisper-soft tickle, gently, so gently, followed by a more resounding lap of the flat of her tongue. Alternating motions have me groaning fiercely. And I shudder and bite down on the sounds that threaten to escape.

"Tell me," she says, her breath a rush of warmth against my wetness.

"Tell you what?" I beg.

"Confess—"

I close my eyes tighter. I can hear the words in my head. It's all about the wanting. Not possessing. Not owning. But the wanting before. And the knowing that I can have whatever I need if I only have the strength to take it. Yet all I manage to whisper are those last words. "Take it—"

"Look at me," she insists, and I open my eyes and stare down at her. "That's what you'll do," she agrees, sounding pleased. "You'll take it for me. Whatever I have to give. Everything I have to give."

Then suddenly I feel the handle of the blade slipped up inside me. She's holding the sharp razor edge in her hand, carefully cradling the scissor-sharp edge as she fucks me with the thick rubber handle. Fucks me hard and seriously. I'm filled by this tool. For once, I'm filled. Does the need lessen? Does the wanting evaporate?

No. Insert a bitter laugh here. No. I just want it more.

In and out, she works the knife within me, pumping her fist against me. I think about that knife concealed in the fleshy softness of her palm. I imagine that her fingers will close tightly—too tightly—around the dagger, and I see in my head the lines that the knife will make. Pure ruby-red liquid squeezing through her fist as she continues to thrust that handle inside me, such a true crimson river that it will seem fake. This is the mental picture that takes me right up to the edge.

"Talk to me," she says again. "Make it real."

"It's a rush," I whisper to her, trying to explain. "It's all about the rush."

Lowering my head to my chest, I start to come. Steady, so steady, causing no sudden movements, the ripples spread through me. So sweetly and quietly those waves spread outward again and again as if they'll never stop. But when I see my reflection in the mirror, I am unsurprised to see that I remain poker-faced. Emotionless. Unchanged until she pulls the knife away from my body, surveys the area of her desire, and makes the first true cut. Only then, when there is no going back, can I give in to her, allowing myself to be caught. And in doing so, allowing myself finally to get free.

OTHER PEOPLE'S PANTIES

Other people's panties turn me on. They always have. Ever since way back when.... In college, whenever my pretty Midwestern roommate was in class, I would dig through her lingerie drawer, fingering the seductive items she was saving to wear when her long-distance boyfriend was in town. Sometimes, I'd dress myself up in her favorite pieces: the matching leopard-print set she thought was particularly racy; or the black lace boy-cut shorts with a tank-style top. Other times, I'd just hold them to my naked body, caressing myself with the fine fabrics. I'd take my time to really smell the material before slipping on the garment, winning a whiff of laundry detergent, perfume, lavender soap, or even the shadowy, lingering scent of real skin.

So I guess that's when it started. My fetish, I mean. Because at some point, wearing Lisa's clothing wasn't quite as important to me as sprawling on my tiny twin bed with the items in hand, stroking myself with the various intricate creations, coming while surrounded by panties and bras and camisoles that weren't mine. That was the key to my pleasure—the panties were someone else's, not purchased by me. Not meant for me. And the owner had no idea of my obsession with her private underthings. No idea at all.

By the end of the year, I had a set routine. Each day, I'd fondle the bikini bottoms Lisa carelessly discarded on the floor by her bed. I'd place them on my face and breathe in while I touched myself, reveling in the ghostly embrace of her, even though I didn't want her. I just wanted her knickers. When the school year ended, my fetish remained. But I learned that I wasn't attached solely to Lisa's lingerie—*any* pretty woman's underthings would work. This is why I've never lived on my own, always have had a female roommate. I've worked to keep my desires hidden through years of flatmates, rifling undetected through laundry baskets, or top dresser drawers, or in the tangle of sheets at the bottom of a bed. My fantasies have deepened as I fingered the sweet-smelling satin hipsters, cotton bikinis, lace thongs. I have succeeded in getting my fill from my female roommates' collections, and I have never once told anyone about my fetish.

Not anyone.

Not even Jamie, my lover who swore on her heart that she'd love me through thick and thin, through sickness and health. I didn't tell her because our commitment ceremony included no line about loving through fetishes, through panty raids, through constant caressing with secreted sexy items. Although I planned to come clean at some point, I found that I couldn't confess. I told myself this was because I didn't know what she would say, didn't know how she might react to my treasured little secret. I pretended I simply couldn't bear to see disgust on her face.

Truthfully?

That wasn't it at all. I just didn't want to stop playing with her panties.

Jamie has perfect lingerie for my needs. She indulges herself in the finest fabrics, the prettiest panties in rainbows of colors. And though I can afford to buy myself the identical items, I know from experience that they wouldn't give me as great a pleasure as wearing Jamie's. Don't know why that is, but I can't change the fact. It's other people's panties that get to me.

If I'm in a pinch, I use a G-string or a thong snagged from the laundry basket, and I go for a quickie while Jamie thinks I'm taking a shower. But when my girlfriend is out for the evening, that's when I truly indulge. I make a whole night out of fucking myself with Jamie's underthings. First, I go through her dresser drawer, or our hamper, and pick out my pieces for the night. Sometimes I get off on a pair of her silky blue hipsters. I breathe in at the crotch. I run my tongue over the seam and taste her there. Or I use her cream-colored, lace-edged tap panties, which I love to watch her wear, but love even more to peel down her long, lean thighs. Occasionally, I dress myself up entirely in her naughty knickers, down to garters and stockings—but usually, it's enough to simply surround myself with an outfit or two, turning the mattress into a display fit for an underwear catalog, writhing around in all her lingerie, basking in the sea of her scent and her seductive taste.

This is all I've done, all I've ever needed—that is, until last night.

Jamie had plans to be out for the evening. As soon as I heard the front door close, I headed down to the bathroom. But this time, I found a surprise when I opened the hamper. Instead of her various clothing items strewn willy-nilly in the basket, they were neatly folded, with a red satin ribbon wrapping them up. I heard a noise behind me, and when I turned around, there was Jamie, waiting, a smile on her face. I didn't know what to say....

"I think they're your favorites," she said, grinning.

My hand fluttered over the blue satin, the soft pink lace, the black see-through thong.

"Yeah," I said, nodding. She was right.

"So take them out. Let me watch. I want to see what you do with them."

"How—" I started.

"Just do it, baby. I want to see."

Trembling, I took the bound package of my treasured items to the bedroom. Then I stripped and started. Jamie stood across the room, watching. At first, I was extremely aware of her staring at me, and I felt a prickle run through my body at the thought of being on display. But then I started to lose myself in the pleasure that always works through my body. I tuned everything out by focusing on the feel of the fabrics and the secret smell of Jamie's own scent embedded in her fine lingerie. I didn't even notice when she came closer and sat on the bed. Didn't tune in to her until she finally moved right next to me, and she took the pieces from me and slowly rubbed them over my body. Everywhere I wanted her to.

And when I came, I whispered, "I didn't know you knew."

I looked at Jamie, into her lavender-blue eyes, at her flushed pink cheeks, and I saw how close she was to coming herself. This was as exciting for her as it was for me—I realized that in a heartbeat—the way she purred back at me. "It turned me on," she said, "when I figured out what you were doing. It made me wet to know that my panties made you wet...."

I guess sometimes you really don't know how another person feels...until you walk a mile—or fuck awhile—in their panties.

LOST IN THE TRANSLATION

W hat did she say?" I whispered to Johnny, staring at the angry flush of heat in Birgit's cheeks.

Johnny shook his head. Together we were lost in a foreign world. Whenever our friends wanted to talk privately, they simply reverted to their native tongue of German, instantly plunging the two of us into helplessness. How could we get involved in a conversation that we didn't understand? So we watched them bleakly, and waited in silence, knowing that eventually they would translate.

This evening, Birgit was the one who finally explained the situation. She wanted to take us out to her favorite restaurant. Wolf wanted to show us the red-light district. The decision was up to us, and there was no way of guessing what had been lost in the translation. As could be expected, Johnny instantly voted for Wolf's plan, squeezing my hand hopefully. I agreed, curious myself, and the four of us drove to the Reeperbahn.

Once there, we wandered along the sidewalks, glancing in shop windows and observing the erotic sights until the harsh throb of a foreign phrase caught my attention. Unlike the flurry of normal conversations floating around us, these words were different, a come-on directed at me.

"What did he say?" I asked Birgit, who had been designated as my perverted tour guide for the evening.

"The women in there," she began, indicating the darkened doorway that led to a hidden strip club, "they're all of legal age. But they're shaved, so they look younger." Then she pulled me along at a trot because we'd fallen behind the boys.

I glanced back at the heavyset barker, who winked at me before continuing his fast-talking German spiel, hawking his human wares to any passersby, even well-dressed girls like us. *What use would we have for shaved strippers?* I wondered, but the sinful gleam in his eyes made me feel instantly dirty, as if he knew all of my secrets. As if he might call them out to the next customer.

Swiftly, we fell into place behind our boyfriends, who were oblivious to the fact that we'd dropped back from them. Both men were fully captivated by the line of attractive prostitutes standing nonchalantly across the street from the police station. Our little foursome was clearly connected, but this didn't stop the hustling women from approaching anyone with a cock. Each girl had a different move—a sensual head nod, a seductive lower lip lick, an air kiss. Some were far bolder than that, stepping forward to actually speak to Johnny and Wolf, making pointed conversation in their lilted, foreign tongue.

"What did *she* say?" I hissed to Birgit after a kitten-like blonde in sleek leopard-print slacks and a zipper-encrusted leather top spoke to my beau.

"She asked if he was interested," Birgit told me, translating the words without hesitation. "She said that she's the best—too good to pass up. Better than his wife." This last bit made Birgit's eyes narrow, as if she couldn't believe the nerve. I watched Johnny carefully for his response. While Wolf rephrased the proposition in English, Johnny looked the prostitute up and down, as if he were actually considering the offer. In my mind, I tried to imagine what Johnny could possibly whisper to me so that I'd let him go and experience "the best."

"We're only here for a few days," he'd say. "And we *did* agree that we wanted to savor all of the international delights before returning home."

Then I'd give him a kiss and tell him, "Sure, baby. Enjoy yourself. Here's a handful of deutschmarks. Have a blow job on me."

As if reading my thoughts, Johnny turned around and gave me a sheepish smile, letting me know that he was simply a tourist on a sex-charged ride. *No problems, honey*, his expression said. *No worries*. On we went, heading toward the main drag of the Reeperbahn, where Birgit told us we could watch dirty movies, visit the erotic art museum, hear a late-night concert, buy a gun, fulfill any one of our decadent appetites. But before we reached the corner, Wolf stopped.

"No, Wilfried," Birgit said immediately. She was calling him by his full name, which showed me how serious she was. "Don't do it."

"He'll never get another chance," Wolf told her.

Birgit shook her head fiercely. Once again, our German hosts engaged in a short, heated discussion in their own language. Johnny and I stood with raised eyebrows and listened to the friends we'd known since grad school. What wouldn't Johnny get a chance to do? And why wouldn't Birgit want him to have that opportunity? Birgit shrugged angrily, as if to say, "Do what you want," and Wolf said in his perfect, unaccented English, "Leave it up to them, right?" and Birgit nodded, blue eyes blazing.

"There's a street," Wolf began. "Where the women are."

I knew that he was leaving out something important, because as far as I could tell, the "women" were everywhere. Turning my head, I spotted several prostitutes moving in our direction. One statuesque brunette was wearing gold hot-pants and lace-up boots, not even shivering while the rest of us were bundled against the chill. Apparently, she had an internal heater. Johnny and I waited silently for further explanation.

"Down there," Wolf said, indicating a glossy, scarlet-painted gate that towered over our heads. "Behind those doors, there is a street where only men can go."

"Why?" I asked, my shoulders tightening automatically.

"They don't want the competition," Birgit explained. "Or simply curiosity-seekers. They want customers. Males mean sales."

"Would you like to go?" Wolf asked. His tone made it apparent that *he* was the one who really wanted to take that stroll. "Just to look," he continued. "They sit in the windows and you choose."

"It's nothing," Birgit said, shaking her head. "Sluts under glass. That's all." But Johnny wanted a peek, I could tell, and so could Wolf. "I hate that we can't go, too," Birgit muttered, revealing genuine frustration. "If they're so good, they should be able to handle another woman walking by."

But they wouldn't want to compete with a girl like Birgit— that was my instant thought. So lovely, with her long blonde hair fanning loose over her black cashmere sweater. Bright blue scarf tight around her throat. Pale blue gloves matching her suede slacks. She was far prettier than any of the stunners we'd seen so far, and she gave Wolf what he wanted for free.

Although, from the furious expression on her face, I thought he
might not be getting any tonight.

Johnny looked at me, a question beating in his deep green
eyes, and I nodded. Who was I to keep him from a once-in-a-
lifetime journey?

"How long will it take?" I asked.

"An hour," Wolf promised. "Maybe less."

He wouldn't meet my gaze as he spoke. Was there something
else in the plan, something that Wolf wasn't telling me?

"We'll see you back at home," Birgit said suddenly, surprising me by how easily she was giving up. "I'm going to take our
little one here out drinking. She's never had a *Hefeweizen,* if
you can believe it. Don't worry. We'll cab." Wolf grinned like
a kid, obviously thrilled that his girlfriend had acquiesced. Had
he never been allowed down the street before? I didn't have time
to ponder that, because the boys were moving in speeded-up
motion before we could change our minds. I watched Wolf open
the red gate, saw the two men disappear behind the wall. Then
Birgit was tugging my hand, pulling me toward a waiting taxi.

"Where's the bar?" I asked as we settled ourselves in the
plush leather interior.

"We're not going to a bar. We're going down that street,"
Birgit said forcefully, her ice-blue eyes gleaming. "It'll just take
a little doing."

Back at their Hamburg apartment, Birgit riffled through Wolf's
wardrobe. "We need guy clothes," she said, "and hats. We're
lucky it's winter. Less exposed skin means less exposed features." I stood, bottle of beer in hand, as I watched her gather
what she wanted. Honestly, I wasn't that interested in seeing
women behind windows, but I was excited at the prospect of
an adventure. Besides, I liked the way Birgit moved, telling me

what to do and how to act. It meant that I didn't have to make
any decisions.

"You'll need to tape those," she told me, indicating my full
chest with a casual motion as she tossed over a roll of bandages.
I'm slim, but I have curves. "Get yourself as flat as you can."

Now that it was really happening, my heart started to race.
Go fast, I thought. *Don't think.* Modestly, I faced away from
her as I pulled off my shirt and sweater and started to roll the
bandage around my breasts. But Birgit moved next to me, help-
ing, her fingers cold on my warm skin as she tucked in the end
of the bandage.

"Wipe off your makeup," she told me. "No lipstick. No
liner." I retreated to the bathroom to follow her orders, then
returned, clean-scrubbed and fresh-smelling, although feeling
something like a mummy in the bandage.

"Perfect," she said. "Now a button-up shirt, I think. Good
that you're so tall. Makes things easier." She cocked her head,
looking me over. "Keep on the jeans, but put on a pair of my
Docs. Your boots are too femme." I followed her commands,
fingers trembling as I did the laces up on her heavy black shoes.
"Leather jacket," she said to herself, nodding. "And some hat.
Baseball hat? Yes, Johnny's got one, right?" As if on automatic
pilot I found myself in the guest room, grabbing Johnny's vintage ball cap from the dresser and putting it on backward.

"Your short hair is a godsend," Birgit said, fussing impatiently with her own intense silky blonde mane. She wrapped it
tightly, tucked the length down her turtleneck collar, and then
grabbed a striped woolen hat. She'd dressed similarly to me, but
without needing to wrap her small breasts. Standing side-by-side
in front of the mirror, we looked like two young boys.

"If anything," she said, "they'll hassle us for being underage.
We need something else." She rummaged a bit more, and then

ran into the kitchen, coming back with a pack of Wolf's Marlboro Reds. Our friends smoke American brands, while we think
we're cool to buy the European ones.

"Smoking will keep our hands busy and give us something to
cover our faces."

Again, we stood in front of the mirror, staring. Then Birgit
snapped her fingers and said, "I know. I know—" and she
reached into Wolf's dresser and pulled out two socks. "Roll
'em up and stick 'em down," she instructed, and soon there
we stood: two insecure youths with smoking habits and serious
hard-ons. "Let's go."

The cab ride was a tense five minutes as I tried to decide
whether or not I could go through with this bizarre charade.
"What happens," I whispered, "if they realize we're girls?"

"They'll throw ice water on us," she said matter-of-factly,
"and bits of garbage."

That sounded like a whole lot of no fun.

"Maybe we should just go to the bar," I suggested softly,
struggling to find a comfortable way to breathe with my chest so
firmly wrapped. "We could have another heffer-whatever—"

"No." Birgit had her mind set. "This is it," she told the cabdriver, and he murmured something back to her as he handed
over the change. Birgit responded with a dark smoky chuckle
that sounded nothing like her normal laugh.

"What did he say?" This was my mantra for the evening.

"He said, 'Have a good night, gentleman,'" Birgit grinned,
pushing me out the door. Then there we were, back in front of
the red gates.

"What if Johnny and Wolf find out?" I asked, my last-ditch
effort to talk sense into my friend.

"What can they possibly say?" she responded. "They've already done it. And who knows what else—"

She was right, and I took a deep breath and followed her through the gate and into another world. Instantly, I saw that we were in a sort of human sex mall. Lining both sides of the narrow street were tiny storefronts with floor-to-ceiling windows. Behind most windows sat a woman, waiting. I was surprised to see that the windows were actually lit with stark red lightbulbs—hence the term *red-light district*. Each window held a comfortable-looking chair, like an old-fashioned recliner. The chairs were decorated in a variety of different styles. Some had flags draped lushly over the seats. Others featured more luxurious fabrics, comforters made of velvet and satin.

As we strolled by, I noticed that several windows were dark. These were the ones that had customers, Birgit explained. "It's early," she said, looking around at the light pedestrian traffic. "Men with their needs come out later in the evening." But although this meant that there were many women for us to look at, this also meant that we were scrutinized as potential customers by each one. Some waved. Some stood in open doorways and beckoned. I could see their eyes, the red embers of their cigarettes, their bodies encased in shiny, revealing clothing.

"Hey, tall dark and handsome, come back—" one called, and I wondered how she knew I spoke English, and then remembered my baseball cap with the SF Giants logo on it. A clever guess. As we wandered, I looked out for Wolf and Johnny, but there was no sight of our mates.

"The boys are long gone," Birgit said. "They scurried down fast."

Turning to look at her, I understood in a mental flash that she was smarter than Wolf, that when he played his little boy games with her, she was always the one in charge. "All macho in front of us," she continued, "but when women are offering sex for real, they get scared."

Maybe, I thought, *but maybe not.* I peered into the hazy gray of one storefront as we strolled by. *Maybe they're each behind one of those darkened windows.*

Because there are things that you can't translate. Expressions. Wounds from old secrets. And there are some things that don't require translation—like the fact that I knew Johnny would sleep with one of the prostitutes if he had the chance, that I knew he'd done so before. Nuances like the heat between me and Birgit, the questioning glances, sly smiles, accidental brushes up against one another. You don't need a phrase book to understand certain concepts even if they are foreign as of yet. Even if you've never done them before.

At the end of the block, we turned around, walking faster down the other side until we reached the starting place. Now that we'd actually succeeded, there was no need to linger. Birgit smiled at me, and herded me through the gate.

"We did it," she said, gripping onto my hand tightly.

My cigarette had burned down to the filter, becoming one long piece of silvery ash. Birgit plucked the butt from my fingers and crushed it out on the concrete sidewalk. Then she took a step closer to me. Her breath was icy. Puffs of wispy frozen air. Behind her, the barker called out to us.

"What did he say?" I asked, desperately.

"He said that his girls inside are young and pretty and shaved." She paused before adding her own opinion in a different tone of voice, "But they're not as pretty as you." As she said the words, she kissed me. Her cold lips pressed to mine, and I felt her arms pull me forward. Wrapped in her tight embrace, I felt her sock cock jammed into my side.

"Is that a tube sock in your pocket?" I whispered, "or are you happy to see me?"

She laughed hard, her real laugh, and then took my hand

again, pulling me back to the taxi stand where a line of cabs
waited. "They won't be back yet," she predicted. "If Wilfried
thinks I took you drinking, then he knows he has a couple of
hours to kick around town with Johnny. They're probably in
one of the kino houses."

"Kino?"

"Movie. *Dirty* movies on this street. Two men, jacking off in
the darkness."

I didn't have to ask what we were going to do. Her fingers
played with mine on the ride home, squeezing. The cabdriver
kept his eyes intently on the rearview mirror, watching.

"He thinks we're fags," Birgit said, pulling her woolen cap
off to reveal her long honey-blonde mane. The driver seemed to
visibly relax. And then Birgit wrapped one arm around my neck
and pulled me in for our second kiss. Sweet, at first, and then hot
as her lips parted and her tongue met mine.

"Here—" she said, just when I was losing myself in the wonder of it all. "Right here." She paid the driver and hurried me
back up the four flights of steps to the apartment. There were
no words then. Just Birgit unwrapping me as if I were a Christmas present. My hat off. Sweater on the floor. Long strand of
bandages unwound and discarded. Shoes pulled free. Jeans in a
faded denim puddle. Birgit took me on the bed, spread me out
on the soft duvet, and started to speak German.

"What—" I begged. "What did *you* say?" Now, I needed to
know. I didn't want to miss any words.

"Relax," she told me, her body soft and warm on mine,
curved and dipping in all the right places. She straddled my
waist and looked down at me, then traced her fingertips along
the line of my forehead, the bridge of my nose, before bringing
them finally down to my mouth. Her fingertips rested on my
lower lip and I drew them in, sucking on two, gently, softly.

I felt the place where our bodies were joined, felt the heat as it seemed to move from her to me. Felt the wetness when it started and I bucked up against her body, letting her know. But she knew. Easily, she moved down, kissing along the rise of my collarbone, down the hollow of my flat belly, making her way to the slicked wet split between my legs.

I thought of Johnny and wondered whether he was behind a smoked-glass door, making love to a stranger. I thought of the barker, offering nubile women for viewing pleasure, or more. And then I thought of nothing, as Birgit spread my nether lips wide open with her slippery fingers and brought her hot mouth against me. She touched my clit gingerly with the tip of her tongue, then ringed it with her parted lips. I felt the wealth of expertise in the way she touched me—she knew what she was doing. Her fingers came into play, holding my lips apart, dancing along the slick wet split. Then she moved her head down and her long hair tickled my inner thighs as she drew a line with her tongue from my pussy to my ass. I groaned and raised my hips, anxious to take whatever she would give.

Mouth glossy, she moved back and forth, licking and sliding, playing tricks and hide-and-seek games with her tongue deep inside of me. I turned my head and stared at the gold-painted wall, seeing our shadows there, growing and stretching with our movements. There were four of us in the room. Me and Birgit, and the two lovers on the wall. When I could take no more, I put my hands on her shoulders and made her look up at me. "Please—" I begged.

"What?" she asked, an echo, a murmur. "What did you say?"

"I want to taste you," I told her, and quickly she swiveled her lithe body around, so that her sex was poised and ready above my waiting mouth. Then we were connected again. My tongue inside her pussy, her whole face against my cunt, pressing hard. I didn't think. There was no need to. I only acted. Lips on her nether lips. Tongue flat to tickle her clit and then long and thin to thrust inside of her. I mimicked each move she made until we were in perfect rhythm. One beast, one being, riding together on that bed.

Nothing has ever felt that good, that right. The way we connected to one another. Skin sliding on skin. Fingers moving, caressing. Searching together to find the end—the answer.

With my eyes shut, I saw the women in the windows, the sluts under glass. With no sound but our hungry breaths, I heard the barker offer up his strippers, smooth and shaved, and then I was coming, and I heard only my heart in my ears as I drove hard against her mouth, sucked hard against her clit, taking her with me, taking her over.

Hours later, the boys found us curled in the bed together, me wearing one of Johnny's shirts, Birgit in one of Wolf's.

"Sleeping off a drunk," chuckled Johnny knowingly as he and Wolf stumbled down the hall toward the tiny kitchen, where I could hear them trying, and failing, to be quiet as they looked for more alcohol. There was a loud bang and then Wolf groaned something in rapid-fire German.

"What did he say?" I asked Birgit, nuzzling my lips against her soft cheek.

"Nothing," she assured me, "nothing important." Her fingers once again found out the secret shaved skin of my bare pussy. Then quietly she spoke to me in German, and I closed my eyes and listened to the delicate murmurings of phrases that I knew promised pleasure, for once not worrying myself about the translation.

THE LINDY
SHARK

With a blare from the slide trombone, Lilly Faye and her Fire-Spittin' Fellas lit into the first number of the evening. Clara rushed to find her place, her polka-dotted dress swirling about her. Within moments she was grabbed around the waist, pulled into a tight embrace, twirled fiercely and without finesse, and then passed to the next man in line. This one had thick, meaty fingers that held her too tightly, creasing the fabric of her carefully ironed dress. She was relieved to be released to the next partner. Her ruffled red panties briefly showed as the third man spun her, dipped her, and passed her on again.

Aside from the briefest of observations, she hardly had time to notice what her partners looked like. Her appraisals were cut short with every turn, only to start fresh with the next. Even when a man did please her, there was no way to act on the attraction. The leader would call out to switch, and she'd be pressed onto the next dancer. Still, she couldn't help but feel a wash of anticipation at the dim prospect that she would be matched with someone who not only suited her moves but also passed her stringent critique system. Although it hadn't happened lately, that didn't mean it couldn't. Maybe *he* would be here again. Perhaps he would notice her this time.

To the sounds of "Jump, Jive, and Wail," Clara found herself with five different men in a row who failed to please her. Handsome, but a poor dancer. Fine looking, but much too short. Sweaty. A groper. Bad, bad hair. Then, finally, as the leader called out for only the experienced Lindy-Hoppers to take the floor, she saw *him*. She watched him move through the crowd with that insolent look on his face. He had heavy-lidded eyes, a tall, sleek body. Like a shark on the prowl, he cut cleanly through the waves of dancers.

"Fine threads," a woman next to Clara said, staring at the man.

"Racket jacket, pulleys, and a dicer," she added.

A little too "in the lingo," thought Clara as she refocused on her dream man—but the woman was right. His vintage zoot suit looked as if it had been tailor-made for him, the suspenders flashed when his coat opened, and the fedora added to his high-class appearance. He had an unreadable expression on his face, a steady gaze that almost seemed to look through her. Then he lifted his chin in her direction, letting her know that he had seen her and approved.

Of course he approved, thought Clara. Her sunset-colored hair, dark red streaked with gold and bronze, was done in pin curls that had taken hours to achieve. She'd applied make-up in the fashion of the era—bright matte lips and plenty of mascara. Her vintage dress was navy with white polka dots, and it cinched tightly around her tiny waist. A pair of stacked heels sturdy enough to dance in, but high enough to make her moves look even more complicated than they were, completed her outfit. She waited for him to come to her side. The girls nearby twittered in hopes that he was coming for one of them.

"I'd let him into my nodbox," one murmured.

A nodbox was a bedroom, and Clara agreed: She'd definitely let this man crease her sheets. She felt like telling the giggling women to give up—the man didn't have eyes for any of them.

He was on his way to Clara.

A rush of nervous excitement pulsed between her legs and flooded outward. Rarely did she feel this self-conscious—normally her moves expressed a quality that came from within, a radiance on the dance floor that couldn't be taught. This man possessed it, too—that's what attracted her. Dancing could be a form of foreplay; she'd always known that. But at most of these swing sessions, there simply wasn't anyone she wanted to take to bed. Sure, she was picky when it came to men—both as dance partners and bed partners. That wasn't a crime, was it? If you chose the right person, for either activity, the results were much more satisfying.

The man reached her side just as a new song began. He didn't say a word, simply put one hand on her waist and steered her onto the floor.

She took her time checking him out. Up close, he was even more attractive. Those dark liquid eyes, like a silent film star's, were infinitely expressive. A deep inky blue, they shone beneath the crystal chandelier. His hands were large and firm, and they maneuvered her with expertise, without roaming where they didn't belong. That was a surprise. Men often took the opportunity to fondle a partner, something Clara generally found distasteful. Now she wouldn't have minded if his hands wandered down a bit, if he tried a little stroking as they glided together on the dance floor.

Clara usually didn't have to think while she danced—her feet easily followed her partner's lead. But this man was making her work, executing several difficult steps from the very beginning, forcing her to concentrate. She forgot about what she hoped he might do to her and focused on keeping up with him.

Other dancers spread out to give them room, as if they sensed something big about to happen. And it was. As the first song blended into a second, and then a third, the duo found their zone. When her partner flipped her into the air, Clara let out a happy little squeal, something totally out of character for her. For the first time, the man smiled. It was as if a marble sculpture had cracked. For the rest of the dance, the moves came naturally. Clara no longer had to second-guess him, to think about where he was going. Instinctively, she followed.

When the music stopped so that Lilly Faye and her Fellas could take a breather, Clara kept following him—down the hallway from the main ballroom and into a small, unisex bathroom. This wasn't something she would normally do, but if he could dance like that, she thought, just imagine how he might make love. He locked the door behind them.

They could hear music drifting in from the ballroom—someone had put on a CD by Big Bad Voodoo Daddy, and it was loud. People headed out to the bar, and voices lifted as spirits flowed. Alcohol mixed with dancing could make people rowdy. Clara was relieved not to be out there with the throng making small talk.

The man lifted her up; she kicked out her heels automatically, as if he were still dancing with her. He wasn't. He set her down on the edge of the blue-and-white tiled sink and cradled her chin in one hand. His full mouth, almost indecently full for a man, came closer. Kissed her. Shivers ran through her body; she closed her eyes and floated on his kiss, not noticing when his fingers moved to the front of her dress and undid the tiny pearl buttons, buttons it had taken her ten minutes to fasten. She remembered standing in her bedroom, looking at her reflection, wondering if this man would be present tonight, if he would like what she was wearing.

Beneath the vintage dress she wore a modern, underwire lace bra and matching panties in crimson silk. The man stroked her breasts through the bra before unfastening the clasp and letting the racy lingerie fall to the floor. When she opened her eyes, she saw their reflection in the mirror across the room. They appeared dream-like, a perfect match. The way it was meant to be.

The man took off his hat and set it on the counter. Then he tilted his head and watched her as she slid out of her dress to stand before him in her ruffled panties, garters, hose, and shoes. Though he didn't speak, he seemed to want her to leave the stockings on. Quickly he turned her so that they faced the mirror above the sink. He lowered her underpants and waited for her to step out of them. She watched in the mirror as he undid his slacks and opened them. She caught a flash of polka-dot boxer shorts that matched her dress—another indication of how perfect they were together.

He leaned against her, the length of his cock pressed to the skin of her heart-shaped ass. The silk of his boxers brushed the backs of her thighs, and she sighed. He gripped her waist, letting her feel just how ready he was. His cock was big and hard, and it moved forward, seeking its destination. Without a word, he slipped it between her thighs, probing her wetness. She'd gotten excited during their dancing; her slick pussy lips easily parted and he slipped inside. Just the head. Just a taste.

The band started up in the other room, and, to the Lindy beat, he began to fuck her. Clara felt as if they were still dancing. Making love to him was as natural as having him flip her in the

air and twirl her around. She opened to his throbbing sex, and
to the insistent beat of the music.

The bathroom's art deco style created a fantasy-like atmosphere, with its blue-toned mirror and tiled walls that echoed
her sighs. Though he remained silent, the man seemed pleased
by the way she moved, rocking her body back and forth, urging
him to deeper penetration. He locked eyes with her in the mirror and, for the second time that evening, smiled. It began at the
corners of his mouth and moved up to sparkle in his eyes. An
intense connection flowed hot between them; she had been right
to wait for him. She felt a sense of destiny as he slid his hands
up her bare arms, stroking her skin, sending tremors through
her body.

She liked the silence, their lack of words. Some boys talked
through the whole thing, ruining it. Lovemaking, Clara felt,
shouldn't be full of chitchat. She craved mystery, magic—and
with him she had it. She felt the same way dancing. Some men
talked when they danced, but if you danced well together, you
could have an entire conversation without once opening your
mouth.

This man seemed to know that. He understood. Not saying
a word as he filled her with his cock, he held her gaze, trailing
his fingers across her breasts, pinching her nipples between his
thumb and forefinger, making her moan and arch her body.

Oh, yes, this was the way to do it, to the sounds of music, in
dim twinkling light. She strove to reach climax in synchronic-
ity with him. She squeezed him tightly with her inner muscles,
watching his face for a reaction.

His eyes closed, long lashes dark against pale skin, strong
jaw set as he held her tight. Yes, it was going to happen. Now.
She closed her eyes, as pulses of pleasure flooded through her,
gripping onto the edge of the sink to hold herself steady.

After he came he didn't withdraw, but remained inside her, growing hard again almost instantaneously. She sighed with pleasure as he extended the ride, this time taking her harder, faster. She felt as if she might literally dissolve with pleasure. Her senses were heightened, and when he brought one hand between her legs, plucking her clit with knowledgeable fingers, she came, biting her bottom lip hard to keep from screaming. She felt weightless, as she had when he'd tossed her into the air. When she looked in the mirror, she seemed transformed, a flush in her cheeks, a glow in her eyes.

She expected him to be transformed as well. After something so spectacular, shouldn't he be? But when he got dressed, he hardly looked rumpled at all, his shirt still cleanly pressed, the fine crease on his pants in place. She felt suddenly exposed, with her bra and panties on the floor, her dress a puddle of polka dots. It would take a bit of work for her to sort herself out. He seemed to understand this, and gave her a final kiss and a wink, and then nodded with his head for her to put on her clothes.

He would meet her outside, she guessed, as she watched him leave, and then hurried to lock the door behind him, her heart pounding like the drum section of Lilly Faye's band. Her fingers trembled as she rebuttoned her dress, the task taking longer than it had earlier in the evening. She kept mis-buttoning and starting again, desperate to finish so that she could get back out on the floor and dance with him again.

Back in the ballroom, she was certain he would hurry to her side, would lift her up in the air again so that her dress would twirl the way it was meant to. Her crimson ruffled panties would show, and the scent of sex would waft around her like perfume. From now on, they would be partnered, showing off for the rest of the crowd. They would go back to her place that night, and in the morning she would take him to her favorite vintage store

on Third Avenue. Would try on clothes for him. Would let him
dress her. There were so many things they could do together.

But when she exited the rest room and saw him standing by
the wall, he didn't seem to notice her. His eyes roamed over the
crowd. She was about to wave her hand, to call out that she was
right here, ready to dance. Then she noticed that the two women
who'd stood next to her earlier were now at the bar across the
way, and the man was heading in their direction. One of the
girls let out a high, flirtatious laugh. The man adjusted his suspenders in a practiced, casual manner and tilted his hat forward
rakishly.

The room blurred before Clara. She saw the truth. Like a
shark, he was moving again through the water of the dancers.
After another kill.

A LESSON IN SEDUCTION

I might just have to let you seduce me."

These were the strangest words a man ever said to me, and the last words I expected to hear from Nick.

"I might just have to let you slide over closer to me and press those pretty lips to my ear and whisper the naughtiest things you can think of."

Me. He was suggesting this concept to *me*. And he wasn't being coy, or sly, or even particularly quiet. In fact, the rock 'n' roll duo at the next booth had obviously heard every word Nick said, because the long-haired blond man turned his head slowly to glance over his shoulder at me. When he saw my shocked expression, he grinned and nudged his dark-haired buddy who turned to look at me, as well.

"What do you mean?" I whispered to Nick, my cheeks scarlet.

"You heard me," he said.

"And so did those rockers." I knew the boys were musicians because they had the prerequisite black T-shirts and colorful tattoos, and because just about everyone at the Rainbow is a musician. The outfits and the fact that two guitars rested in the spots where their dates should have been clued me in. Since sleek-looking, dark-featured Nick was a musician too, he fit perfectly into the atmosphere. I was the odd girl out, a writer instead of a player. So why was I struggling so hard for words? Easy enough to answer that one: Nick left me speechless.

My crush didn't seem to care that the headbangers had heard him. He put one strong arm around my shoulder and pulled me even closer to his side. I could feel our hips press together, our legs align themselves with each other, and I basked in his heat and his closeness. Even though this was our first date, I felt comfortable in his presence, but that didn't make his request any easier. Not for a shy girl like me.

The truth is that I've always had a thing for listening. If a boyfriend says that he wants to kiss my neck, or strip me naked, or use a blindfold to cover my dark green eyes, I'm halfway to the finish before we even start. I love to hear dirty words whispered in a husky voice, but mostly, I like to star in X-rated make-believe worlds, described to me in delicious detail by a bawdy bedtime partner.

This is why I was sure Nick was my perfect man. He always had something to say. He was a singer and a deejay and I'd seen him work a crowd before a concert and give witty off-the-cuff interviews. There was no way he wouldn't be able to satisfy my desires. In fact, I had it all worked out in my head. During dinner, he'd lean in to tell me each and every action he planned on doing to me later in the evening. My panties would be sopping before we finished our meal.

Yet, he had his own plans for the evening.

"You want to, Samantha," he said, "isn't that right? You want to tell me all the secret fantasies that fill your thoughts at night. The sexy things you think about when you touch yourself in bed."

Finally, I found my voice. "Yes—"

The blond rocker looked over his shoulder at me again and said, "You're going to have to talk a bit louder than that for us to hear you, sweetheart. They've got the music cranked up too fucking loud tonight—"

But that bit was just in my head. The tattooed musician *did* look my way, and this time he gave me an encouraging wink before nudging his friend again. Customers are like that at the Rainbow. Everyone wants to know everyone else's business, and the dark cherry-red leather booths are situated close enough for people to easily eavesdrop. I've been at the joint late at night when strangers actually share pizzas, passing slices over the booths and taking bites off other people's forks. "Trade you a slice of Hawaiian for a slice of pepperoni." Crazy. But that's L.A. for you. We may curse at each other when we're on the freeway, but we're all part of one big fucked-up family.

This scenario tonight was classic Hollywood, with Nick's roaming fingers running up and down my arm, and his hot breath against my neck as he continued to tell me how *I* was the one who was going to seduce *him*. His hand slid over my breasts and he squeezed each one gently, instantly making my nipples hard through the filmy material of my halter. This evening, I wore a skimpy petal-pink top with my faded 501s, and I'd dusted blush between my breasts to deepen the valley and draw Nick's attention there. My trick had worked. Nick palmed both of my breasts, and I moaned out loud, loving how firmly he touched me. The sound surprised me, and I sat up straight, but I knew that nobody was concerned about the fact that we were canoodling in the booth. Waitresses have seen worse at the Rainbow.

Much, *much* worse.

I must say here that this scenario wasn't my style at all. Yes, I may have an extremely dirty mind. In fact, I might have already fucked Nick twelve-thousand times before, all in my head, with my legs spread, fingers, dildo, or shower massager playing over my clit. But I hadn't told him that, and I didn't think I could. He had other ideas on the subject entirely. He seemed to believe that I was some sort of she-cat, able to stalk her prey…with words if not actions.

"You tell me," he said.

"Tell you what?"

The rocker leaned over the booth and said, "Tell him how you want to fuck him, doll baby. Tell him that you think about his steel-like cock parting your nether lips and sliding inside where you are all warm, and wet, and ready. Tell him that late at night, you envision him slipping a black velvet blindfold over your gorgeous green eyes and taking you from behind, doggie-style, so he can get in deep. That's how I'd fuck you, if you want to know the truth. That's how every man in this joint would fuck you. Because you like it doggie-style, don't you, kiddo? So a man can pull your hair and take charge of you. Yeah, I can tell. You have that look—" but again, that part of the conversation occurred only in my imagination.

"Tell me everything," Nick suggested.

"Oh," I said. "Everything. That's easy enough. Just, you know, *everything*."

"*You* asked *me* here, Sam," Nick reminded me, "right?"

That part was true. After months of crushing on this guy, I'd finally gotten up the nerve to ask him out for pizza. I'd thought that if he saw my interest in him, he'd do the rest. Apparently, my life wasn't going to work out like a B-movie plot on Lifetime for women. I was going to have to do more than simply set the script in motion.

"All right," I said, feeling his warm fingers find the button fly of my jeans and slide in between the row of shiny gold buttons. He started to stroke me gently, as if I were his instrument, and I felt my body automatically respond. My thong was drenched in seconds, and if Nick's probing fingers had fully split the fly of my jeans and probed southward, he'd have found that out for himself. "Sure, I'll seduce you," I said, using the most confident tone I could manage.

Immediately, I heard the rockers snicker, this noise not in my head at all. Maybe my statement was a little too matter-of-fact to be sexy. Maybe she-cats aren't supposed to announce their intentions to their prey in the style of a waitress stating, "I'm Brittney and I'll be your server tonight." But suddenly, there in the dimly lit Rainbow, surrounded by pictures of my musical idols, I found my sex appeal.

The way to seduce this man, I decided, was to come clean. To tell him everything I wanted, and to let him listen. I was going to give him a first-class aural experience—him and the rock 'n' rollers who had pressed themselves as close to our booth as they possibly could. They'd completely stopped their own conversation, not even pretending any more that they weren't listening to us.

Nervously, I pushed my long dark hair away from my face and leaned in even tighter against Nick. My skin was sun-kissed from a day out at Malibu, and I could feel the heat still beating on my bare shoulders and at the hollow of my neck. "Here's the thing," I whispered. "I've been dreaming about you since I first saw you." No, that was all wrong. "I mean," I continued, "I've been dreaming about fucking you—"

That won me a deep intake of breath from Mr. Blond Rocker, whose attitude let me know that he didn't think I had it in me to say a four-letter word. I looked too sweet, I supposed. Too nice and young and naive. But even sweet girls like to fuck every once in a while, or twice in a while. And this sweet girl in particular was very ready to fuck the man at her side, regardless of whether the musicians were listening in or not. This particular sweet girl was already desperately wet, shifting on the leather seat to gain deeper connection to her date's fingertips. Nick let his finger graze over my panty-clad clit, and I almost cried out at the instant wave of pleasure that flared through me.

"Since that first time?" Nick prompted.

"Yeah," I nodded weakly. I thought of the offices at the alternative entertainment newspaper where I work, the courtyard below that houses a music agency. And I thought of catching a glimpse of Nick wandering into the agent's office, seeing his fine figure in the dark jeans and black T-shirt. Knowing, somehow, that it was his custom Harley parked out there on Westwood Boulevard. I'd grown accustomed to his visits, and I'd made myself known to him, as well. We have upstairs and downstairs offices, and I began to run errands between the two whenever I heard his bike pull up. I saw him watch me, and I watched him back, and then finally, I asked him to the Rainbow.

"Because," I told him now, "I want you to bend me over, and fuck me."

"Here?" He seemed to find the idea charming.

"Here," I repeated, and the dark-haired rocker grinned at me, and would not look away. If I was going to get fucked on this table, then he was going to have a front-row seat. He'd call out encouraging comments. Or maybe he'd get involved, his fingers reaching out to stroke my hair out of my eyes or pinch my nipples, or lean in to graze my ass. He might bite my bottom lip

hard, or he might throw money on the table, as if we were putting on a show for his pleasure.

"On this table?"

"Yeah," I said, firmly, "on this table."

Nick chuckled, and I'm sure he saw the vision in his mind. I
wanted him to. I wanted him to see me, stripped down and bent
over, while he plunged into me from behind.

"Look, I know it won't happen at the Rainbow," I said
softly. "But that's what I fantasize about."

"So tell me."

"So I am," I laughed, suddenly feeling more confident from
the way his fingers continued their tantalizing caresses over my
thighs and then back to my button fly, teasing me once again by
sliding in between the row of buttons to touch my naked skin.
"When I saw you that first day, I imagined you walking up the
stairs, entering the office and stripping me naked. I saw it in my
head—saw you putting me up in that picture window, fucking
me from behind so that everyone could see. My hands flat on
the pane of glass. My ass pressed against you. I imagined all the
people on their commute along Westwood Boulevard getting the
show of their lives. Watching the two of us fuck."

"That's what I thought, too," he admitted, "when I saw you,
I thought—just do her here. Mount her here. Now."

"And the next time," I told him, "when I saw you park your
bike, I had a different X-rated vision entirely."

"You bent over the seat—" he nodded before I could say it.
"I'd pull your jeans down your thighs, and you wouldn't have
any panties on underneath. I'd touch you to see if you were wet
and my fingers would come away sopping—" Somehow, I realized we were now playing each other—both equal partners. Our
audience was clearly spellbound, not moving now in case they
broke the enchantment. They were visibly having the best time

listening, and I realized with a shock that I was having the best time performing for an audience of three.

"I'd never been on a Harley," I told him, but I thought of you taking me up to Griffith Park and then fucking me over your bike."

"You like to say the word *fuck.*"

"I like the action even more than the word."

"I thought writers were more inclined to use a variety of terms. You keep repeating that same one over and over."

"Because that's what I want," I told him. "I know all the euphemisms, but I don't want you to 'make love' to me. And I don't want you to 'do' me. Or 'take' me. Or 'ravish' me." I drew a deep breath before saying this last part slowly and emphatically: "I just want you to fuck me."

Confession time was over.

Nick pulled me to him and kissed me, his strong chest pressed against mine, hands sliding up and down my arms. "Yeah," he said softly as we parted. "Yeah, Sammy. That's what I'd like to do, too." I felt tremors run through me at his kiss, and I forgot to keep myself in check. I moaned louder as he moved his lips down in a line along my throat to the dip of my cleavage, and then I slid my own hand under the table to feel Nick's cock through his jeans.

He was hard. As hard as I'd hoped he'd be. Harder, even. I thought of his bike out back behind the Roxy, the club right next door where we were supposed to go after dinner. And I realized we weren't going to make the show, but that we might make a show of our own.

The musicians stood up then and threw money down on their Formica table for the beautiful blonde waitress who has been a fixture at the Rainbow for at least twenty years.

"She did good, Nicky," the blond one said as he walked by the table. "She seduced you all right—"

"And us, too—" the dark-haired one added.

"What do you mean?" I stammered, startled by their boldness.

"Don't be embarrassed, sweetheart," the blond told me with a wink, and then he put enough money on our table to cover our meal as well.

I stared after the rockers as they left the restaurant, and then turned to look at Nick, confused for a moment before I got it. They were his friends. Made perfect sense, didn't it? We were here, at the rock 'n' roll hangout in Hollywood, where everyone knows everybody else. These musicians would be going to the show next door to see their buddies play. The Rainbow is the natural stop for anyone who's in the mood for a bite before heading out to the strip.

"You knew they were listening, and you let me talk like that."

"You knew they were listening, too—" He was right. I did. "And it turned you on, didn't it? All that dirty talking in front of a willing audience."

I nodded.

"But we don't need any audience anymore, do we?"

"No, Nick."

"And we don't need to play make-believe in this booth anymore either."

I shook my head as he took my hand and led me out to the parking lot, whispering to me as we walked. "But I don't want you to stop talking, baby," he said. "I want you to keep whispering those pretty little secrets to me—which is exactly what you've wanted to do all this time, isn't it?"

I'd been found out, a secret desire uncovered, which was far sexier than my original plan for the date of having Nick seduce me. As sexy as Nick driving up to the hills in Hollywood and spreading his battered leather jacket out on the ground and fucking me—not taking me, not doing me, not making love to me, just fucking me.

I felt the firm ground beneath me, felt the bed of grass under my ass and Nick's hard body on mine. I closed my eyes and thought of all the visions I'd had of him, the months spent fantasizing, and now here we were. Fucking for real. Nick brought his lips to my ear as he worked me. He took over, doing what I'd thought he would the whole time, telling me everything.

"You're so nice and tight," he crooned to me. "Squeeze me like that, baby." I did as he said, and he continued, "Oh, god, just like that."

I contracted on him, helplessly, as he lifted me up, switching locations so that he was on his back and I was astride him, my halter the only item of clothing left on my body, my nipples like pebbles beneath the filmy material. A cool night breeze stirred the leaves in the trees around us, but our bodies stayed warm from the heat of one another. As I moved myself on Nick's cock, I found that I couldn't stop talking, either.

"You knew they were there," I said, smiling. "You liked them hearing."

"I wanted to see how far you'd go."

"How far?"

"Just far enough," he said, and he slid a hand between us as I pumped my thighs, and his thumb found out my clit and stroked it up and down, then in a circle, then just pressed hard, giving me exactly the contact I needed.

I could feel the silent shudders work through my body. Looking down at Nick, I felt my hips work faster, felt the passion take over, so that I wasn't thinking anymore, I was letting the sensations happen to me. We had that unbelievable connection, where everything clicks. How wet I was, how hard he was, how he knew to draw me down against him, so that my breasts were pressed against his chest, so that he could grip into me, bite into me with his teeth on my shoulder.

I cried out, so hungry, so happy, as I began coming on him. The world felt still around us. The stars were obscured by the lights of L.A. I heard the melody of traffic down below, the endless hustle that is never entirely stilled in Hollywood. But there was silence close around us, and noise further off, and then the almost indecipherable sound of skin on skin, as we slid together. He whispered something under his breath as he came.

"Talk to me, baby. Talk to me."

And I did.

I'd been quiet for so long. His lesson in seduction had given me a voice.

THREE IN ONE

It happens so quickly that I don't know what to do. I have my hands inside my panties, touching myself with random, randy circles. Then suddenly, a second set of hands are on me, covering my eyes, and before I can fully react to that unexpectedly erotic development, yet another set of hands joins in, forcing my hands out of my satin bikini bottoms and touching my pussy for me.

I think it's a woman behind me and a man down below, only because of the softness of the hands covering my eyes and the roughness of those yanking my pretty pearly-white panties down my thighs and then spreading my pussy lips wide apart. I feel how exposed I am, and I would blush if I had the time. But everything happens so quickly that I don't respond in any normal fashion. I don't scream. I don't fight. Not when the blindfold covers my eyes. Not when the feminine hands begin to pinch my nipples, making them tent the slinky fabric of my semi-sheer T-shirt. I simply relax, relishing every second of the illicit experience. I groan as those rougher and ever-so-insistent hands on my sex stretch me wide and then wider, and I moan out loud when I feel a wet smear of lube drenching my inner lips.

"Oh, fuck me," I sigh, so wet, so very ready. "Please, fuck me—"

But although those hands are busy working me, nobody says a word. Fingers thrust forcefully into my pussy, and I clench down hard and lift my hips high in the air, savoring every second. I'm in heaven, the roughness of those hands palpating my clit takes me on a delicious ride, alternating perfectly with the tightness of thumb and finger on my nipples pinching ever harder. Hands caress me, rub over me, massage me.

"Oh, god," I sigh, right before a large, hard cock finds my mouth. Now, my moans and sighs are muffled by the rigid tool, but at least I have something to do, some sort of purpose. I start to suck on the cock, focusing on the way it feels, the way I instinctively know how to swallow on it. I'm so overwhelmed by the pleasure of submitting that it takes me a moment before I realize that a second cock is filling my pussy. Christ, so it was two men. One more feminine, perhaps, than the other. But that's okay. I'm ready. I can take them. I suck and suck, working the cock down my throat, and I can fuck and fuck, my pussy contracting on the cock inside me, bucking and thrusting, lost in this visionless world until…I feel a finger probing my asshole.

My body tenses. I'm scared at the intrusion, and I feel goose bumps rising on my skin. A chill flutters through me, shaking my entire body, but the finger is gentle, so gentle, and I sense the wetness of lube skating around my tender rear hole. Around the cock, my mouth forms an excited O, and I rock back slowly, impaling myself on the probing digit.

Yes, I think. *Finger-fuck me there.* As if the unseen lover can read my mind, the finger obeys immediately, finger-fucking my asshole while my pussy is all stuffed full of cock. I'm going to explode, filled in three places, but I love every fucking second. The cock in my mouth thrusts deeper, faster, and I know I'm going to drain every drop. The hard member in my pussy works at a steadier rhythm, a deep thrust in, and then out, and then it holds totally still while that finger goes into play again. But now, there's a second finger, pushing forward, overlapping, and I cry out around the cock in my mouth at how good that feels.

Oh, do I love a finger in my ass. Especially one so well-lubed and so slow to proceed. I'm going to come. I can sense it. I'm going to come in ribbons of pleasure, in waves of power. My invisible lover understands this, and the cock in my cunt pulls out and starts to gently fuck my clit, slipping back and forth in my ocean of wetness. I find that I'm on the verge of both creaming and screaming as that cock finds the rhythm I need. Now, the owner of those venturing fingers in my ass starts to fuck me faster, working at a delicious pace.

I'm such a slut, I think, raising my thighs up in the air, holding them in place, spreading myself, my rear cheeks, so that the finger can drive in further. *Look,* I want to say. *Look at me here. See everything. I'm spreading myself. I'm revealing myself. Look at my asshole while you touch it.*

The cock in my mouth and the one on my clit both fuck me until I come, shuddering and sighing, nearly sobbing. And as soon as I start to come, the cock at my clit slides down lower, and hands force me to roll onto my stomach. I turn my head carefully, still sucking the cock in my mouth, as the one behind me starts to press forward, butting against my rear hole. I shake my head forcibly, never relinquishing my hold on the cock I'm blowing, but I don't mean it. I don't mean "no." I want to come again. I'm a greedy little thing. I want to contract on that cock. I want to feel it in my asshole.

Slowly, so slowly, the cockhead teases its way in. I clench my eyes tight, and then the bulbous head is in me. I sigh with relief as the shaft slides easily forward.

Oh, yes. Oh, yes. I'm going to come again. This time with the cock in my asshole. I use my own fingers under my body to touch my clit while I'm getting a pounding in my rear hole. My fingers work faster; the cock thrusts harder, and then I'm there—at the finish, panting and sweating, and so high from the release that I let the cock slip from my mouth.

After a moment, I push the blindfold away, only to discover that I am alone in my bed. There are no strangers making love to me, only a few soiled dildos and a half-empty bottle of lube on the mattress at my side. I'm all by myself.

I grin when I think about tomorrow night. When I just might go for three in one once again.

THE LAST DEDUCTION

An audit. A tax fucking audit. Nadine couldn't believe it. She'd filed her forms on time, didn't make a shitload of money, kept careful—well, adequate—records of her expenditures. Why was the IRS harassing her?

"They always go after the little guys," her friend Daphne explained, "waitresses, like me, or freelancers, like you. They know you're too poor to afford an expensive accountant and that you'll probably be too scared to challenge anything that they say." Daphne shot Nadine a sympathetic look. "You'll be fine, hon. You're so honest. I'm sure they won't find anything out of place."

"But I don't have all my receipts," Nadine confessed, impatiently brushing her dark hair out of her eyes. "I mean, I have a whole shoe box full of scraps of paper—"

"Give *that* to the auditor," Daphne said righteously. "Make him work for it."

"And some of my deductions might be a little—" Nadine's voice trailed off.

"A little what?"

To answer the question, Nadine pulled open the doors to the closet where she kept her writing materials. Like a hostess on some X-rated game show, she pointed to a battery-powered vibrator with harness, a bone-handled crop, and a pair of high-heeled fuck-me pumps with tiny studded ankle straps that glistened in the light.

"You put *those* on your itemized return?"

Nadine nodded.

"Under what heading?" Daphne snorted. "Office supplies?"

"Miscellaneous research items," Nadine said, adding emphatically, "I used everything here for my latest book. Every single piece."

"And I'll bet Steven loved each minute of it," Daphne said as she stood to take a closer peek, her green eyes wide in disbelief.

"Forget Steven," Nadine said, "help me figure out how I'm going to explain what I do to a tax auditor."

"You're a writer. Tell him that you need a wide variety of experiences in order to get in touch with your characters." Now Daphne was slipping into a pair of bright red feather-tipped mules and admiring the way they looked on her delicate feet. "Did you write these off, too?"

"Of course. They were for a story called 'The Death of the Marabou Slippers.' "

"I wish I could be there," Daphne said, looking longingly at the pink and black rubber-coated paddle, the thick silver handcuffs, the ball gag. "I can just imagine the guy's face when you show him what's behind door number one." She started to laugh. But Nadine didn't think it was funny.

Was it really necessary to have bought all the different toys? Nadine debated the question, because it was one that the auditor would undoubtedly ask her. If she were a mystery novelist writing about a murder, would she go buy a gun? No, but she most definitely would hit the shooting range. Pump round after round of ammo into some defenseless piece of paper. To her way of thinking, that sort of quest for knowledge was the equivalent to slipping a plastic butt plug up her heart-shaped ass before trying to write about what that experience felt like.

Besides, her ex-boyfriend had loved it. At least, at first. As she prepared for the audit, she thought about the different kinky times they'd shared together. With Steven starring in the role of her personal sex slave, she'd experimented with a whole assortment of erotic toys. Acting the part of a dominant woman wasn't unique for her. She had done that from time to time, anyway, taking charge, being on top. But pushing the limits of that fantasy, getting down and dirty without fear of reprisals—well, that's where the real research came into play.

Closing her eyes, she remembered the time she'd fucked Steven with a massive black strap-on cock. Made to look anatomically correct, the tool was ribbed with veins and sported a rounded mushroom head. Just sliding the accompanying leather harness around her slender waist had turned her on. Having Steven on his hands and knees getting the head of the plastic prick all dripping with his mouth had made her knees weak. That was something she'd never have known if they hadn't played the scene out together. She'd been forced to pull herself together, to act the tough, female dom. Telling him to get as much spit on her tool as he could, because she was going to ream his ass when he was finished. It had been difficult for her not to stop mid-scene and write down dialogue for her book, but she'd managed to wait until he'd come.

Extreme.

That's what the experience had been. And it was why the two had ultimately broken up. She couldn't shake the pleasure at being on top. No reason to go back to anything else. She wanted the power—and, oh, did she have it when she put on her slick, expensive boots, when she wielded the toys that Daphne had so tentatively pointed to.

Yet how was she going to explain all of that to a tax auditor?

"Ms. Daniels?" the man in the suit asked, arriving right on time on the dedicated day. The meeting was taking place at her beachfront condominium, because Nadine worked at home. "I'm Connor Monroe," the man continued. "Your auditor."

My auditor, Nadine thought, irritated by the man's clean-cut good looks, the Boy Scout quality of his carefully pressed suit and polished leather shoes. She was especially irritated because she found him appealing. Connor Monroe seemed more like a male model than someone who served the government in its most hated capacity. If *she* were to create a character who worked for the IRS, she'd have made him heavy, balding, old. Not Connor. He had short dark hair, stone-colored eyes, and a sleek, athletic build that was apparent even with his suit on. In other circumstances, Nadine would definitely have flirted with him, batting her long eyelashes over her deep blue eyes, stroking one hand sensuously along the curve of her hip to give him ideas. She knew all of the ways to behave in order to make a man want her, but this wasn't the time.

Holding open the front door to her apartment, Nadine tried to put a pleasant expression on her face. "This way," she said, "I have my papers in the bedroom."

Inwardly, she smirked at his obvious hesitation, letting him suffer for a moment in silence before continuing. "That's where my office is. I'm not rich enough to afford a two-bedroom condo yet." Why not let him know that she was angry? He couldn't penalize her for a bad attitude, could he?

As the man followed after her down the hallway, he spoke, sounding as if he were repeating a memorized line from a script. "I know an audit is a frightening proposition for some people. But it's just a regular practice at the bureau. Not any sort of punishment. Think of this as a routine, like an annual visit to the doctor."

Nadine let herself smile since he couldn't see her face. In her research closet, she had lots of toys for "doctor" visits. A box of regulation rubber gloves. A naughty nurse's uniform. A real stethoscope. Playing doctor was something she knew a lot about. She thought about one of her last nights with Steven. How she'd examined him, spread his handsome rear cheeks open as if to take his temperature, and then tongue-fucked his ass until he'd shot his load on her mattress, creating a little lake of cum beneath his flat belly. No need to share that bit of information with Mr. Uptight IRS Man.

"Here we are," she said, opening the door to her room and gesturing inside. In preparation for the meeting, Nadine had made her bed neatly, the black satin comforter hiding the evidence of her silk leopard-print sheets—another write-off. The room looked as utilitarian as it possibly could with her paperwork spread out on her writing desk. What receipts she did have were well-ordered, and the shoe box was there as well, lid on firmly to hide the mess contained inside. Wasn't that an echo of every part of Nadine's life? The surface looked one way—but take off the lid and see the inner turmoil within.

Regardless of her attempts to make the place look more official, it was obviously the bedroom of someone who liked sex. A dusky, romantic room, with flocked wallpaper and feminine touches in the prints on the walls and the rose-colored rug on the hardwood floor. The auditor, *her* auditor, looked around, taking in the intricate brass frame on her bed, the two candelabras that stood on small round tables nearby, perfect for wax play when she was in that sort of a mood. How she liked to tilt the candlestick, to let the hot liquid wax drip in pretty patterns along a naked chest—

She shook her head, trying to clear the image of doing such a dirty thing with the tax man. He was here to discuss her payments...not her panties. Still, she wondered whether he was feeling a pull between them, as well. Or did she just have sex on the brain because she'd been looking in her research closet prior to the audit?

"I'm not out to ruin your day, Ms. Daniels. We really had only a few questions," the auditor said, sitting at Nadine's antique desk and waiting while she perched on the edge of her bed. He opened his leather briefcase and pulled out a copy of her tax return, pointing to several lines that were highlighted in bright yellow ink. "And, honestly, the problem wasn't that we didn't agree with the deductions, it was that we didn't understand them."

He smiled again, and Nadine thought she saw something shimmer in his eyes. A look that didn't match the Boy Scout image at all. His expression made her feel flushed, and she looked away.

"Vagueness is something the IRS can't handle," he continued, self-deprecatingly. "We expect things to fit into neat categories. Phone. Entertainment. Rent. Travel. So, this $6500 deducted for 'Miscellaneous Research Supplies.' That raised a red flag."

Nadine sighed, her worst fears realized so quickly in the afternoon. She was going to have to open her toy chest and reveal the different items she'd used as the foundation for her latest X-rated sex novel. Might as well get it over with quickly. Without a word, she stood, walked to the closet, and pulled open both of the mirrored doors.

"I'm an author," she explained, lifting the different implements and placing them on her comforter, one after another, as casually as if they were pens and paper, any other equipment of a serious writer. "I throw myself into my work, learning every aspect of my characters' lives. My most recent novel took place in an S/M environment." Carefully, she set out the high-end vinyl dress, the handcuffs she'd bought for the equivalent of a month's rent, the shoes with heels so high they couldn't possibly be walked in. But that was okay, since they weren't created for walking. She noticed that the auditor's eyes had opened wider, but he didn't speak.

"If I were writing about pet care, I'd buy grooming materials. If I needed to learn about the art world, I'd have purchased books about Monet and Picasso. I hope you're not going to judge me based on the content on my work."

The auditor had stood and was now observing the growing pile of items on Nadine's bed at closer range. She noticed that he had the same look on his face that Daphne'd had when she'd picked through the toys. Intrigue rather than disgust. She also thought she saw a bulge in his trousers that hadn't been there before.

"Do you understand now, Mr. Monroe?" Nadine asked, her husky voice low. "I had to file everything under 'miscellaneous,' because the IRS doesn't provide neat categories for whips and chains. For bondage gear. For handcuffs—" As she said the word, he hefted the pair, interrupting her.

"Connor," he said softly.

"Excuse me?"

"My name's Connor. You don't have to call me Mr. Monroe."

Connor. She liked that. And she also liked the way he was

playing with her toys, rifling through them as if with a private purpose, stroking the shiny material of the vinyl dress—perfect for water sports—holding up her corset and then looking at her, as if picturing her in it. "This is all for a book?"

She nodded. "*Paradise Lounge*. It will be out next month."

"And your character is—"

"A dominatrix," she said, and again she noticed that flicker in his eyes. Was he getting turned on? She found that *she* was, and she shifted in her faded jeans, feeling suddenly too constrained. As she watched, Connor slid one of the cuffs around his wrist and closed it. Then he looked at her.

"I think I understand now," he said, "but maybe you could explain what you do a little more in depth for me. So I get the full picture. I'm a bit anal that way. I like to possess all of the facts before I write up my reports."

Nadine didn't need any more encouragement. She felt the heat between them, and she recognized fully the looks he was giving her. "Strip," she said sternly, without hesitation. "You don't want me to mess with your nice, expensive suit." Connor did as he was told, like a good boy, and the metal of the handcuff chain made music as he took off his jacket, shirt, and tie, then kicked off his slacks, socks, and shoes.

"Boxers, too," she said, admiring him for a moment. My, but he had a fine body, even better than she'd expected. Tightly muscled legs, flat stomach, and, most importantly for Nadine's particular fixation, a round firm ass. "You can't really appreciate the image I'm going to create for you unless you give yourself over to it totally. That's how it is for me, anyway. I lose myself in my characters. Plunge hard and deep until the rest of the world disappears."

With his eyes locked on hers, Connor slid off his boxers and then stood, waiting. Oh, he was erect. So hard that Nadine felt a moment of weakness. What she would have liked to do was go on her knees in front of it. Meeting a new cock for the first time was always an exciting prospect. Nadine adored that initial taste, learning how the man's bulbous head would fit into her mouth, stroking the underside with the tip of her tongue, gripping into his ass to pull him forward, harder, at her pace. But not yet, she reminded herself. Take your time. Play it out.

Steeling her inner yearnings, she took hold of the other handcuff, pulled the man forcefully onto her bed, threaded the chain through the headboard, and captured his free wrist. He allowed himself to be manipulated without a word, letting Nadine know that he understood she was in charge.

"Now," she said, "you want a demonstration of my research equipment."

"No," he shook his head, then motioned to the rock-hard monument between his legs. "A demonstration of your mouth."

That made Nadine smile, her cherry-red lips curving upward at the corners. The man had attitude, which she appreciated. But she wasn't about to reward him from the start. Where was the fun in that? No, she wanted to make him pay for the fear she'd had from the moment the IRS had contacted her. That starkly written letter sending panic through her. Nadine hated to feel panic.

"We don't play that way," she said. "Not by your rules. But by mine."

"And they are?"

"That's the fun part," Nadine grinned, stripping out of her own clothes and sliding into the short vinyl dress and her favorite pair of leather boots, feeling the power start to build within her. She sensed that Connor was memorizing the look of her body nearly naked, but she didn't give him a long time to observe her. "You get to figure out the rules as we go along."

Connor tilted his head at her, as if he didn't know what she meant.

"You ought to comprehend that concept," she said snidely. "Isn't it how the IRS works? Secret rules that you auditors get while the rest of us poor people are forced to guess what on earth will make you happy?"

But what would make Nadine happy?

She considered the question as she glanced over her implements of pleasure and pain. Her auditor continued to watch as she hefted the different devices. The strap-on cock. Yes, she'd had fun with that in the past. Steven liked to be taken, bent over the bed and thrust into, his asscheeks spread wide, the only lube a bit of spit that Nadine worked up and down the rubber dildo with the palm of her hand, jerking the cock the way a man would.

"Was that one of the items on your tax return?" Connor asked meekly.

Nadine nodded. "Used it for research for chapter twelve."

Next, there was the wooden paddle, perfect for heating the ass of a naughty boy. This particular paddle had a satisfying weight in her hand, and she considered it with an almost loving expression, remembering the scene she had written with the paddle virtually the star of the chapter. She thought of the night she'd tested it on Steven, actually bringing him to tears before letting him come.

"And that was in the miscellaneous items, as well?" Connor asked. Nadine heard the note of fear in his voice, but gave him extra points for staying in control of himself. He didn't ask whether she would use the paddle on him, didn't beg her not to. She nodded in answer before moving on to an oily looking

black leather belt, slipping it between her fingers and then leaning forward to use the very lip of it to tickle Connor's balls. He
arched his back at the move, and a bit of precum made the tip of
his cock seem to shine.

It wouldn't take much to push him over the edge, Nadine
knew. She could do just about anything, and he would cream
for her. Yet she wanted to have some fun, to make the experience worthwhile. Finally, she decided on one of her five-star
toys: a vibrating wand shaped like a cock. Once it was combined with a little of the lube she always kept in her bedside
table, she would enjoy introducing this pin-striped man into the
world of submission.

"Roll over," she said.

He tilted his head at her and rattled the chains, indicating
that he couldn't.

"Don't mess with me, Connor. There's enough slack," she
said knowingly. "It might hurt a little bit, the chain rubbing into
your wrists, but you can do it."

Obediently, Connor followed the order, twisting his body
onto his stomach, shifting as if to make room on the mattress
for his erection. Then shifting again because it was obvious he
liked the friction.

"None of that," Nadine said fiercely, her open hand connecting with his ass in a stinging slap. "You get off when I tell you.
If I tell you. Not before. Understand?"

Connor sighed but said nothing.

"Do you understand?" Nadine repeated slowly. "That's rule
number one. I'll give that one to you for free. You answer when
spoken to."

"Yes, Ms. Daniels," Connor said, voice slightly muffled.
Mmm. He was learning already. Not calling her by her first
name. Choosing "Ms." instead of "Miss." Nadine lifted the

leather harness that went with this particular sex toy, and fit the large synthetic cock into its resting place. Then she fastened the harness around her slim hips. She did the work behind Connor, so he couldn't see her, could only hear the metal of the buckle connecting. Having a cock on always made Nadine feel different inside. Gave her a little bit of a swagger. But there was still plenty of woman in her, and she wouldn't start with poor Connor without giving him the foreplay he might need before she fucked him.

On hands and knees behind her auditor, she held open his firm bumcheeks and licked once up and down between them, then made a tight, hungry circle right around the velvety rim. Connor sighed and ground his hips again into the mattress, but this time, Nadine didn't tell him to stop. Instead, making her tongue hard and long, she pointed it and drove it home.

"Oh, Christ," Connor groaned, thrusting hard against the bed.

She didn't have to ask whether he liked it. The way he moved made it obvious that he wanted her to fuck his ass and he wanted her to do it now. Sure, sometimes she would play longer, make the guy deep-throat her massive hard-on before screwing him. But this afternoon Nadine couldn't wait. She wanted the feeling of gripping into his shoulders and sliding the length of her cock deep inside of him. First, she reached over Connor's body, opening the drawer on her bedside table and snagging the bottle of lube. Kindly, she spread it the length of her pinkish cock, her fingers working it and getting extra grease on the tip. To prepare him, she slid two fingers into his ass, opening him up. Teasing him a bit with the intrusion.

"Please—" he said, and she knew somehow that he meant to say "please stop." This was all far too new for young Mr. Monroe. The fact that he didn't continue with the request let her know that he didn't want her to stop. Not really. And he didn't have the balls yet to say, "Please fuck me." So he left it just at that one word. Nadine didn't mind. With both hands, she spread him even wider apart, then placed the huge, knobby head of her joystick at the entrance of his ass.

An evil grin on her lovely face, she found herself repeating the same speech, altered only slightly, that he had given her upon his arrival. "I know an ass-fucking is a frightening proposition for some people. But it's just a regular practice in my boudoir. Not any sort of punishment. Think of this as a routine, like a visit to the doctor." Then she reached for the remote control device that went with the toy, holding it tightly in one hand. Now, she was ready.

As she slid the cock in, the power flooded through her. Jesus, but she loved taking a man. In the oval-shaped mirror over her bed, she saw the way she looked as she fucked him. Her glossy dark hair framed her pale face, and her eyes turned a smoldering blue of the ocean in turbulent weather. With one hand on his waist to keep herself steady, she made the ride last. Giving him a taste, then pulling back. Slamming in deeper, and holding it. Connor let her know the rhythm that he liked based on the sounds of his moans and the way he echoed her thrusts with his body against her comforter. He was going to come all over it, make a sticky white pool on the black satin, but she didn't care. Because once he got off, she had other plans. Methods to make this afternoon last.

It had been way too long since her last fuck.

Taking Connor hard, she used her free hand to reach around her until she found the mess of toys still spread out on the bed. Her fingers brushed against the handle of the wooden paddle and she hefted it, such a nice weight, and then let the weapon connect with Connor's right cheek, leaving a purplish blush there. Pretty color. She gave the left cheek a matching blow to even out the hue, and as Connor started to moan, she kept up the spanking. That sound was such a turn-on. The clapping noise, like applause, of a sturdy paddle meeting a naked bottom. She continued to both fuck and punish him until he said, "I'm going to come, Nadine—" a perfect time to switch to her first name. Made it seem that much more personal. "Now."

With those words, Nadine hit the button on the remote, and the cock inside Connor's asshole began to move, startling him as those sexy vibrations worked through his body. "Oh, fucking god," he groaned. He arched and then shuddered, his whole body releasing, and Nadine threw herself against him, still inside deep, so that he felt the length of her body pressed into his skin. In this position, the base of the vibrator buzzed against her clit, sending her wet pussy into spasms that lasted as long as she kept her cunt pushed forward. Oh, yes, that was perfect, the pleasure that had kept her on edge as she was fucking him now spread throughout her body, making her skin tingle in waves that radiated outward from the hot zone between her legs.

Sealed deep into Connor's ass, her hair spread out over his shoulders, her vinyl-clad breasts pressed into his back, she held him. This was the way she liked to be held when she came during anal sex. It was comforting, soothing, to be wrapped in another's arms. But after a moment, she pulled out, tore off the harness, and stripped.

Out of breath, Connor rolled over on the bed, chains clinking, and watched her. Even lost in the postclimax bliss, it was obvious that he was admiring the curves of her body, her flushed perfect skin. Nadine felt his eyes on her, but didn't pose for him. She was busy planning round number two. Naked, she stood in front of her closet, and then she found what she was looking for.

"What's that?" Connor asked, pointing as Nadine lifted the bone-handled crop with the braided leather tip.

"This?" Nadine repeated softly as she approached him. "This is my last deduction."

YOU CAN'T ALWAYS GET WHAT YOU WANT

Trust me. You can't. At least, not when what you want is a firm and powerful over-the-knee spanking from your deliciously strict boyfriend, and he's half a world away from you in a place you'd never heard of before he announced he was about to leave.

"Georgia," you said when he broke the news. "That's not so bad. I can visit."

"No, not *Georgia*—Georgia," he told you, smiling without being condescending in the least, without saying, "What the *fuck*, baby? Did you sleep through geography class?" Instead, he petted your dark hair and kissed your soft lips and said, "Not Georgia-Georgia, but Tbilisi. Kazakhstan. Azerbaijan. Turkmenistan. Former Soviet Union. *That* Georgia."

And you blushed a rosy pink and tossed your glossy dark hair and said, "Oh, right. *That* Georgia." As if you knew all along—but you didn't. (Though suddenly that line about Georgia from "Back in the USSR" made sense.)

So no, you can't always get what you want. Because when your man is somewhere you've never heard of, and you're all by yourself in an apartment that seems much too large, what you want seems as far away as he is. Add in the fact that all you can get is phone sex disturbed by constant static and an air of confusion between the two of you because what's "night" to you is "day" to him, and vice versa.

"Come on," you said, yearning for release, "please Sam, please tell me what you'd do if I were there."

"Baby, I'm at work. You have to call me later. Call me tonight and I promise I'll take care of you."

"It *is* tonight," you insisted. "It is very tonight, Sam." The sky was dark outside your window. You tried to imagine him beneath a sunlit blue sky.

"Then call me tomorrow—"

Sometimes, you can't even get what you need, when what you need and what you want vie for attention in your head until you are nearly crazy with desire, constantly shifting, moving your body to find a comfortable position that has eluded you for the four months, three weeks, and six days since he left. Nothing is comfortable, because your ass isn't freshly spanked and your pussy hasn't been sweetly fucked, and you haven't given a blow job that lasted until your jaw ached. Comfortable is no longer comfortable.

With your eyes shut, you fiercely tried to get yourself off.

Christ, kid, you knew how to masturbate before you met him. Why couldn't you do it now? There should be no difference. Your fingers still made those lulling circles. Your vibrator still used two C batteries. Your stash of porn rested in its special place, in a floral hatbox under your bed. What was the problem?

You needed him.

You wanted him.

You craved him.

But phone calls to Tbilisi cost more than twelve dollars a minute, and you agreed that you would only talk occasionally, using email the rest of the time. When you made that plan, you didn't know that email hadn't come to his job site. So you broke down and made a few phone calls, and those became marathon sessions in which you confessed that you might actually be losing it here.

Because here's the thing—when it costs twelve dollars a minute to talk, it's difficult to relax enough to get off. And when you *can* forget the cost, crashed out on your bed after several stiff drinks, touching yourself as you beg him to tell you what he so desperately wants to do to you when he gets back in town, well, it's lunchtime for him—so you can see how that might pose a problem.

"Please," you begged. "Christ, Sam, tell me—"

"You know, baby. I'd give you the spanking of your life."

"Tell me more."

"Your red ass growing redder by the second."

"Oh, yes—"

"And... Oh, shit, baby. The other line is beeping."

"Ignore it."

"Could be work."

But it never is. The other line is always for his roommate, whose name is something like Zeno or Zero or Zorro, and whenever *he* gets on the phone, he refuses to get off. So you can't get what you want—which is uninterrupted phone sex. And your man can't get what he *needs*, which is uninterrupted sleep, because bands of starving dogs roam the streets, and thugs with machine guns find it amusing to demolish Pepsi cans with their ammo, and happy drunks—after running out of friends and family to toast—noisily exit the bars to toast the local trees.

By the time Sam arrived back in the States, he'd lost fifteen pounds, a bit of his sanity, and every last ounce of willpower. He'd promised you from a pay phone during a stopover at the airport in New York City that he was going to do two things before you even left the airport: fuck your ass, and spank your bottom until it was raw and red and cherry-perfect. You couldn't have been more excited to have both of those things happen.

Finally, you were going to get what you wanted! He was going to quick-step you back to the truck and take care of you in the way you'd been dreaming of for months now. But when Sam walked up the ramp, everything changed. He didn't smile. He didn't kiss you. He grabbed your hand and dragged you outside, into the muggy Los Angeles air. He chose a spot behind a pillar, where a concrete planter was half-filled with dying flowers. He set down his huge camping-style backpack filled with all of his possessions from his trip, filled with everything he hadn't given away to people who needed things more than he did, if you want to talk just a little bit about "need"—and he sat down on the edge of the planter, hauled you over his lap and lifted your silly little Catholic schoolgirl skirt that you'd thought he'd find so sexy. While taxis vied for curb space, he pulled your white panties down your thighs and began to punish your ass for you right there, on the cigarette butt-littered sidewalk of LAX. And you thought for about half a second that you were in public with your bare-naked ass showing, and you thought for another half a second that someone was going to call the police or that people were going to complain.

And then Sam wrapped his hand in your hair and pushed your head down and continued to spank your ass in rapid, smarting strokes until you forgot to think about anything except the pain flaring through you and the fact that you'd been longing for a real spanking, not a pat-a-cake spanking, but a real, serious spanking for what felt like ever.

Still, you had some sense of decorum left in you, and you said, "Sam, the truck's just over—"

"Bad girls get punished in public all the time," Sam hissed, interrupting you. "Nobody says anything about it. Why should anyone say anything about you? Besides, people see worse every day in Los Angeles."

And you supposed he was right, because nobody did anything. Yes, you were behind a pillar, but only barely. Anyone could see if they thought to look. People walked right on by as his hand continued to spank you, over and over again, marking you, bruising your pale skin, and somehow you just forgot about yourself, about your need to be refined and present a certain appearance to the world. You'd wanted this feeling of surrender for months, and you gave in to the sensation, so that you actually came when his fingers spanked between your cheeks to touch your pussy. And then, after letting you vibrate for several seconds with the climax, Sam thrust you off his lap, grabbed his overstuffed backpack and said, "Where's the truck?"

You tried to pull up your panties, but Sam shook his head.

"Leave them."

"What?"

"Step out of them and leave them."

And despite thoughts of littering and being disrespectful to the Earth, you still couldn't be disrespectful to Sam, so you stepped out of your panties and looked down at the shiny white silk you were about to discard as Sam repeated, "Where's the truck?"

You were turned around, your head all happily hazy, and you had to think for a moment before nodding toward the structure across the street. Sam led, even though he didn't know where you'd parked, but in moments you'd found the red truck, all shiny from a recent detail job, and the two of you got in the back, where you'd put a blanket out, thinking that this might actually happen.

Now that he'd spanked you while pedestrians and commuters could see, you felt much less worried as he pushed your skirt up to your hips, reached for the lube you'd also put out in the truck bed, and began oiling up your asshole for you. His pants were open and his cock was out, and you watched over your shoulder as he jacked himself with another handful of the lube.

"Take your skirt all the way off."

With fumbling fingers you searched for the zip, then heard a rip as Sam "took" the skirt off for you. Then his weight was on top of you, pushing you down, and you felt his firm hands parting your asscheeks, felt his cock press forward and then thrust in. You screamed, but the sound was muffled by the blanket. You thought of the fact that you'd circled for half an hour before finding this out-of-the-way corner of the parking structure, but still, anyone walking back here would see you rutting together—and maybe that was something that you both wanted and needed to know.

He fucked your ass the way he always did, with his fingers gripping your waist and his mouth finding the ridge of your shoulder through your sheer white top, biting you hard as he fucked you harder. You sensed when he was going to come, and you slid your own hand down under your body and thought about all the times you'd tried to get off while he was gone, unable to talk him to orgasm, unable to reach one yourself. You thought about wants and needs and desires. Your finger tricked over your pulsing, swollen clit, and you thought about the thugs with machine guns still roaming the streets and you wondered if anyone was ever able to come in Tbilisi. But that didn't matter, right? All that mattered was that you and Sam were about to come, right now, in the back of your 4X4, and he was going to fill your asshole with his seed so that it would slowly seep out of you over the next few hours, and when you got back to the privacy of your apartment, much kinkier things were going to happen to you. That was for sure.

And then he came, and you came, and you rolled over and looked at him, love in your eyes, before you each wiped off on the blanket and you did your best to put your skirt back together, but failed. In order to leave the parking lot, you had to hand over your ticket and pay for the time spent. The man in the tiny booth looked at the two of you. Sam had been up for more than twenty-six hours. You no longer had on a skirt or panties.

"Pleasant trip?" he asked.

Pleasant trip. The words echoed in your head. He'd been gone too long. That's what had happened. That's what had gotten you to this point. A crazy, uncaring point. He'd gone to a place where drunken men toasted trees, where his roommate— Zero? Zorro? Zeno?—barked at you when you called too late, where email didn't exist, where neither of you could come.

Pleasant trip.

You couldn't hold up the line of traffic explaining to this man that *pleasant* wasn't quite the right word, but Sam just laughed. "Not this time," he said.

And the ticket taker laughed back and said, "Well, you can't always get what you want."

You couldn't believe it, couldn't believe he was so accurately putting into words what you'd thought about for months, but Sam just nodded as you pulled the truck out onto the busy L.A. thoroughfare, as if he couldn't agree more.

"But if you try sometimes—" you started to say.

Sam finished it up for you with his standard, trademark sinful smile: "You just might get what you need."

PAGE TEN OF
THE EMPLOYEE
HANDBOOK

We should stop," you say in that semisweet, semismug tone of yours. "Really, we should." I can tell from the taunting look in your lovely large eyes exactly how you want me to respond. I don't need any additional hints, but you continue as if I do. "It's against the rules," you add, gazing down at the floor as if shocked by your own naughty behavior.

"What is?" I ask, softly. "This?"

"Oh, yes," you tell me, playing coy now. "That's just wrong, wrong, wrong."

Now, I press you up against the wall of your office so that your palms are splayed flat on the wood-paneled wall. Then I slide that short black skirt up past your curvaceous hips. I take my time, because I like to admire the view. "Or this?" I whisper to you, my mouth against your neck, teeth poised and ready to bite. You can feel my hot breath on your skin and that makes you tremble.

"That," you insist. "That's just flat-out unacceptable."

"Ah," I sigh. "This is all getting clearer to me. You're saying that I'm just not supposed to do this—" As I speak, I gently slip your lilac satin panties aside. I love these panties. The black lace trim is a total turn-on, and the way they perfectly and snugly fit your ass drives me wild. I know that you wore them for me, and that makes me even harder. The image of you looking through all of the naughty knickers in your collection before choosing this particular set gives me pleasure.

Even though I do love occasionally absconding with your panties, slipping them into a jacket pocket to take home and play with later—this afternoon, I don't take them down, just push the smooth, slippery fabric out of my way, and my finger-tips play out an immediate melody over your clit. For a moment, I make you lose your cool. My fingers stroke and tap, and you suck in your breath at the first wave of pleasure. .

You can't be so clever now, can you? Not as the shining wet-ness coats my fingers, as I push back up and stand next to you, staring directly at you as I lick your juices off the tips.

"Oh, god," you groan. You can't suppress the shudder that throbs through you as you watch. Don't you love the way that looks? Me slowly, so slowly, tonguing away your sweet nectar.

"Is *this* wrong?" I ask, reaching my hand up under your skirt again to collect a fresh dose of your honeyed juices on the tips of my fingers. The first taste of you has made me hungry for more.

"No, don't stop—"

At your request, my fingers probe deeper, and I hold on to you with one hand, keeping you steady as I finger-fuck that sweet pussy of yours. I want you to be ripe and ready for me by the time I take my cock out. You need all the lubrication you can get, because I'm going to fuck you hard. Even harder than you're thinking about right now. I'm going to slam you up against the wall and make you forget how to be coy. How to tease me with those bedroom eyes of yours. Or should I call them "boardroom eyes"?

"I don't know," I say, dropping to my knees and bringing my face right up to your cunt. I breathe in, adoring the smell of your sex. The scent makes me dizzy with need. "If employees aren't supposed to date, then you probably shouldn't let me lick your pussy."

"Doesn't say anything about that—" you assure me in a rush.

"What do you mean?" I tease. "What are you implying? That we should sidestep the rules? That wouldn't be fair to the rest of the workforce, would it?"

"I'm just saying—" you start, but then you can't finish your thought because my tongue is already tripping along the seam of your body, playing you so sweetly. I know how to take care of you. I know the little tricks that you like best. My tongue makes several smooth rotations right around your clit, not actually touching that hot little gem, just brushing around it carefully. Slowly. And then, right when you think you're going to die if I don't touch you where you want, I slide my tongue along your clit in one long brushstroke. You grip into my hair and hold on, shivering, so close already that I'm sure you can imagine exactly how good it's going to feel when I let you come. But I'm not letting you. Not yet. With a slow and steady pace, I resume those lazy, crazy, everlasting circles that make you want to sprawl out on the plushly carpeted floor and let me just lick you for hours.

"So," I say, speaking right up against your most tender skin. "What would page ten have to say about this—"

"No, nothing, nothing," you whisper, and it sounds as if you're begging. You're the one who brought it up, though. Remember that when I make you bite down on your lip to stifle your screams of pleasure. You're the one who opened the manual and used a bright lemon-yellow highlighter pen to illuminate all the different rules that we were breaking.

I can tell now that you're dangerously close, and so I stand up despite your whimper of protest, and I push against you. This is my favorite way to fuck, driving in from behind with both of us standing, but at first I simply let you feel my cock against you through my clothes. I want you to know precisely how excited I am. How ready I am for you. When you whimper again, I rip open my fly and pull out my rod. You're in the perfect position, back arched, poised to receive me. I wrap one hand around your mane of dark hair and tilt your head back so that I can watch your face as I slide inside you. That first deep push is unlike any other sensation. The way your body surrounds me is sublime.

God, are you lovely. Your eyes grow wider at the moment of penetration, and then get a faraway look, as if you've just arrived at some wonderful distant location. That exotic location called "I've almost reached it." We both know all about that place. And I'm going to take you even further—to a tropical island called "coming together."

Out in the hall, I can hear the bustle of secretaries working. Hear the voices and the sounds of their fingers on the keyboards. Their chitchat on the telephones. I hear the low, gruff talk as different employees hurry past the room. Everyone's busy. Everyone needs something. Nobody will bother us, though. That's not even a tiny worry on my radar screen. Officially, we're holding a meeting, the two of us—an important, private meeting—so we can take our time.

Our time to do all the things I need to do to you. And I need to do so many things. Rutting forward. Driving hard. I need to make you crazy with the fact that you can't make noise. You can't be loud.

I want you to be warm and pliant, relaxed and ready, for what we're going to do next. Because this is what I think about it all, baby—if we're going to break those boundaries, we might as well do it right. Might as well really get down to business. Don't you agree?

VIEW FROM PARIS

The view from the balcony overlooking Paris's residential 13th *Arrondissement* took in romantic rooftops, a breathtaking candy-pink sunset, and a lone young man in a firecracker-red T-shirt watching the two of us with unwavering interest. Josh saw him first. "Look down, Lanie," he said, his hand under the strap of my gauzy silver nightgown. "Over there..."

I looked in the direction he was indicating, and that's exactly the moment when Josh slid the straps over my bare arms and pulled my forties-style movie-star nightgown past my naked breasts to the curve of my hips.

"Josh..." I said, crossing my arms over my full breasts. "He's watching."

"That's what I was telling you," my new husband said, nuzzling the back of my neck as his hands removed mine from my breasts. His fingers took over, teasing my nipples as he continued to kiss along the nape of my neck. "He's been there every evening."

And so had we. This was our new tradition, to slip into nightclothes in the late afternoon, waking just when the sun went down to catch a sunset romp out on the balcony. We'd felt exposed, yet oddly protected, being up on the fifth floor of the apartment we'd rented for our honeymoon. Now I knew that we weren't protected at all. Josh seemed thrilled by this prospect, and as his fingers relentlessly played over my breasts, I relaxed into the idea, as well. We were in Paris, after all. Nobody knew us. None of our normal, everyday activities were in play here. Our entire routine was topsy-turvy in the most pleasurable way. We no longer started our morning with a healthy meal of oatmeal and OJ. In Paris, we had croissants at ten, then lingered over filling lunches around one, not bothering to even think about dinner until nine in the evening. At the time of day when we'd usually be facing rush hour traffic, we made love.

Now Josh moved to my side and turned me so that I was facing him. We were still easily visible to our naughty neighbor, and I kept that in mind as Josh began to kiss my breasts. He used one hand to palm my right tit while he suckled from the left. Then he switched activities, so no part of my body felt left out. As his mouth worked me over, I thought about the scene we'd admired the night before. Josh had suggested an evening at The Crazy Horse, and we'd enjoyed the erotic art of the women dancing and exposing themselves to us. Was I crazy enough on Paris's open attitudes to let myself be a woman on display? It seemed that I was.

When I didn't protest, or try to pull Josh back into the apartment, he slowly undid the tie at the back of my nightgown that held the dainty fabric in place at my hips. With one pull of the lace, the nightgown slid in a ripple of lovely silk to my ankles. Here I was, a woman of satiny skin and curves, bathed in the pink glow of the heavens and admired by two sets of eyes: my husband's and those of the man in the bright red shirt. And while I've always adored being on display for my man, it was the stranger's eyes that made me tremble.

Who was he? What did he think about my body? Was he turned on by my feminine curves or by Josh's hard and lean physique?

These thoughts and a multitude of others were still running through my mind when Josh bent me over the railing and began to kiss between my thighs from behind. I felt the slight breath of cool evening air surround me and the warmth of his tongue and lips against my pussy. The sensations were intensely arousing—being outside while behaving in the most intimate of ways has always been a turn-on for me, a fantasy I don't usually get to indulge in. Josh and I live in such a small town that the disgrace of being caught playing in public would be too much to live down. Too much for us to ever get more frisky than a little petting in a parking lot every once in a while.

But we weren't in our small town anymore. We were in Paris, and I gazed into the room owned by a stranger and imagined I could see the yearning in his face, the desire in his eyes, the bulge in his slacks.

Josh made me thoroughly wet with his naughty kissing games, and then he stood and slid his pajama bottoms down, parted my thighs, and entered me. I closed my eyes for one moment, basking in the dreamy feeling of being taken by my husband. But I had to open them again quickly so that I could stare at our audience. I've read that when you're on stage, you're supposed to choose one person to focus on, and do your show for that single selected audience member. I'd chosen mine, and he seemed deeply honored, leaning into his windowsill, anxious to catch every act of our very personal show.

My handsome husband fucked me from behind for as long as

he could take it, and then turned me around, lifting me into his embrace and bouncing me up and down on his glorious cock. I couldn't watch from this position, but I didn't mind. I could feel the stranger's eyes on my body, and my pussy responded by tightening and releasing rapidly, connecting with Josh, contracting on him.

When I came, it was as if there were three of us right there on the balcony: me and Josh and a man whose name I didn't know, but whose willing participation took me higher than I ever had been before. I cried out, not bothering to try to stifle the sounds of my pleasure, and Josh responded by coming right away, holding me tightly to his body as he filled me up. We stayed connected, my legs around his waist, until a shiver ran through me and Josh set me down on the tiny balcony once again.

As I reached for my discarded nightgown, I thought about our choices for honeymoon locations, and our decision to come to Paris, a place renowned for its sights. It turns out the most exciting view Paris had to offer was us.

ON FINDING JON'S PORN

It was for a homework assignment. The simplest kind, and therefore, the easiest to forget. My computer died midway through on the night before deadline. The globe with a tiny question mark inside turned around and around. Rebooting only seemed to make it madder. I know I could have gone to the student center and rented time on a computer there, but I was lazy. Instead, I sat on the edge of my twin bed in a sulk, kicking the metal bed frame like a four year old who didn't want to take a nap. Over and over my bare heel connected with the metal, creating a satisfying thud each time. I might have spent the entire night like that if Jon hadn't stopped by and taken the time to ask me what was wrong.

"Deadline," I told him, "and dead computer." I gestured hopelessly to the ever-spinning globe on my screen. Round and round and round it went. Mesmerizing. Dizzying.

"Take my laptop," Jon offered immediately. "No problem. I'll print your paper for you when you're finished."

I gazed up at him, realizing that this meant I actually had to get back to work. "You're a lifesaver," I told him, only half-kidding.

"You haven't heard what my payment is going to be," he grinned at me.

I typed in the first half of the paper from scratch, and then, feeling as if I'd been wasting my time doing the same thing twice, I started to poke around on his computer. Like I said, I was lazy. Besides, Jon's files seemed way more interesting than my paper on the floor pattern of Prussian churches.

On finding Jon's porn, I knew that my evening was going to end decidedly differently than it had started. On finding Jon's porn, I discovered that Jon was an entirely different person than I had thought he was when we started.

He looked like a choirboy. White blond hair, pale blue eyes, a Brooks Brothers sense of style in an Urban Outfitter world. His dorm room was always clean and neat, to the point of being obsessively so. I didn't know anyone else who sent his shirts out for laundering, not any junior in college, anyway, nor any other student who owned his own vacuum. He was a Third—as in, Jonathan Elliot Dawson the Third—and he had an unshakable vision of his future. One that he would share with his closest friends. One that involved a top-floor office, a forty-foot yacht, and a vacation home on Lake Arrowhead.

But what I now discovered to my great shock and darkly twisted satisfaction was that he also had a massive, overpowering, intoxicating collection of raw, stark porn downloaded from the Internet. My eyes scanned picture after picture, rabidly, hungrily. I felt myself growing ever more aroused, and I started typing with only one hand, so that I could cradle my pussy with the other, pressing two fingers directly against my clit through my faded old jeans.

Unlike Jon's other female friends, the ones who lived in so-
rority houses and wore matching pastel sweater sets, I was far
more Aaardvark's Odd Ark than Ann Taylor. I possessed a vintage aesthetic that led me to wear perhaps a bit more black than
I should have. My glasses sported rhinestones on their catlike
corners. My shoe collection ranged from spectators to bowling.
An odder couple you wouldn't easily find—but Jon and I were
tight friends. The type to stay up late over coffee and discuss our
future. The type to lend a computer to a chum in need.

Might we be more than friends? I'd never considered the possibility before. Had I been lazy in that respect, too?

When Jon stopped by to see how the paper was progress-
ing, I didn't even pretend not to have found his stash. I glanced
over my shoulder, and then back at the screen, waiting to see
what he'd say. What he'd do. Would he flush in embarrassment,
mortified by what I had found? Or would he dredge up a quick
lie, claiming that the pictures were someone else's? That his
roommate, Lawrence, had borrowed his Powerbook and had
taken the time to download the thousands of pictures I'd had
the luck to discover? Or would he become self-righteous? What
in the hell was I doing looking through his personal belongings,
rifling through file after file, my sticky fingerprints all over the
keyboard, hot and wet?

He did none of those things. Instead, he came to stand behind
my desk chair and set his large, strong hands on my shoulders
and leaned forward, looking at the pictures with me. I could feel
his body behind mine, and I paid attention to him in a way I
never had before.

"That—" he said, tapping the screen lightly with one finger.
"That one's my favorite."

I could have guessed.

All were specific photos, specifically anal, and this particular picture showed a man parting a girl's rear cheeks and lubing her up with a torrent of clear K-Y. You could see her puckered asshole, shaved, beautiful. You could see how rock-hard he was, and you could just guess what it was going to feel like when he filled her. Or, at least, *I* could.

"Do you like it, too?" he asked.

I nodded. "Close the door—"

"Your roommate—" he reminded me.

"Out of town—"

"Do you have—"

All of our sentences were like this. Disjointed. Rushed. Yet perfectly clear to the two of us, and that's all that mattered.

"Yeah," I told him, squirming out from between the chair and the desk to pull open the drawer at the side of my tiny twin bed. He wanted lube. I had lube. He wanted more than that—I was stripping before he could even tell me what to do. It was obvious, wasn't it? He wanted me naked, spread out on my bed, my ass toward him. And I wanted that, too.

I watched over my shoulder as Jon undressed. He took off his clothes far more slowly than I had, surveying the scene in front of him with a look of total contentment on his face. Total control. Next to me was the computer, with the image of the lovely young model showing off her perfect asshole. And on the left was me, doing just the same exact thing, as if Jon had down-loaded me from the website.

"God, you're beautiful," he said, his breath against my spine. "I've been fantasizing about this for months—"

And then his mouth was lower, moving swiftly to kiss be-tween my rear cheeks, licking and tickling me as he readied me for step two. But he didn't hurry the foreplay. I wouldn't have thought he would. Not after looking at all of those pictures. He seemed like someone who definitely wanted to build up to the climax. How he built managed to surprise me even more.

"You didn't finish your paper, did you?" he whispered, his mouth against me.

I shook my head.

"You decided to be a little snoop instead." In between his words, his tongue worked magic over me. He traced it up and down between the crack of my ass, and then he plunged forward. I don't think I'd ever been that turned on before. I was dripping wet from my foray through his gallery of porn. Now, with his mouth on me, I knew I was only seconds from coming.

"A snoop who could use a little discipline—" he hissed, and I shuddered all over. Something seemed to snap in me as Jon pushed me down on the mattress and held me pinned there, like a butterfly, beating uselessly to get free. He used his bare hand on my ass, smacking my right cheek and then my left, repeatedly punishing me while he spoke. I stared at the girl on the screen. She could use a spanking, too, couldn't she? I stared over my shoulder at Jon, my eyes moist, my pussy far wetter. How had he known? How could he tell?

The sounds of our dorm mates echoed down the halls. Were they having yet another shaving cream fight? How totally juvenile. Jon and I were the adults. Or rather, he was, spanking my tail until I started to moan, and then returning to his previous mission, spreading apart my asscheeks and sliding his cock into my rear hole.

While I looked at the picture on his screen, he rode me, as hard as I'd ever been taken. He fucked me like all the lovely girls on the computer were getting fucked. And I came like them—powerfully, uncontrollably. Shocked at myself. And shocked at Jon.

You see, on finding Jon's porn, I realized that I was definitely going to miss my deadline—but I wasn't concerned about that any longer.

Sometimes deadlines are worth missing. Sometimes secrets are worth sharing. Jon's collection was just such a secret—one we kept between us for the rest of the year.

THE SUPER

His wife-beater T-shirt caught my eye first. The tight-ribbed cotton showed off his muscular arms and broad chest. I turned slightly to look at him, my hand on the small copper mailbox key, my whole body still like a deer appraising the chances of crossing the street safely. If he noticed me, would that be a good thing or a bad thing? The connection happened suddenly. His eyes made forceful contact with my legs, and I felt each moment as he took his time appraising my outfit: slim short skirt in classic Burberry "Nova" plaid, opaque black stockings, shiny patent leather penny loafers, and lace shirt with a Johnny collar that was probably a bit too sheer for work, but I paired it with a skimpy peach-colored camisole and nobody said anything. Maybe somebody should have.

He did.

"Wore that to work today, did you?"

I blushed, instantly, automatically, and pretended there was

dire importance in the action of checking my mail. My fingers
felt slippery on the multitude of magazines and catalogs stuffed
inside the tiny box, and I hoped I wouldn't drop the whole
handful of mail. I could feel him moving closer, and now I could
smell him, as well. Some masculine scent, mentholated shaving
cream, or aftershave. Not cologne. Wouldn't be his style.

His hands were on me now, thick fingers smoothing the collar of the shirt, then caressing the nape of my neck, his thumb
running up and down until I leaned my head back against his
large hand. Crazy, right? In the lobby of the apartment building,
letting this man touch me. But I couldn't help myself.

"A little slutty," he said, "don't you think?"

My mind reeled at the insult. Slutty? The entire outfit cost
more than a thousand dollars. The skirt alone was worth nearly
half of that. Now, his hand became a fist around my hair, gath-
ering my black-cherry curls into a makeshift ponytail and holding me tight.

"Don't you think?" he repeated, his voice tighter, as tight as
his fist around my long hair. With his free hand, he pushed my
mail back into the box and flipped shut the door. I dropped my
hands to my sides, not needing to pretend to busy myself any
longer.

"Yes," I murmured, agreeing suddenly. It *was* slutty, the skirt
far too short for a professional woman, the shirt sheer enough
to be lingerie. The whole outfit was much more appropriate for
bedroom games than office politics. What had I been thinking
when I got dressed that morning?

"Yes—" he repeated, his voice tighter still.

"Yes, Sir," came as automatically as my agreement, as automatically as my feet began to move as he pushed me forward to
the apartment at the end of the long, narrow hallway. I stumbled
once on the blue- and maroon-colored Oriental runner, but he

caught me, his other hand high up on my arm, so firmly gripping me that I could feel the indents of his fingers digging into my skin. I'd have marks, I knew it, dark purple bruises showing each place his fingers made contact, but I said nothing.

He hurried me through the door to the living room, then kicked the door closed and hauled me quickly to the sofa. I saw everything swirling around me. The chocolate leather of the sofa, the bare shiny wood of the floor. He sat down and looked at me, and I shifted uncomfortably before him. I knew better than to sit, knew better than to do anything but wait. Yet waiting was the worst. Waiting and wondering. And hoping.

Of course, hoping—

"Dressed like a naughty little schoolgirl," he hissed through his teeth. "Dressed in public like that," he continued, shaking his head now, as if he couldn't fucking believe it.

I looked down at my feet, head bowed, curls falling free now around my face, and all I could see were my polished loafers and his scuffed work boots, the dark denim blue of his Levis, the wood floor....

"Do you have anything to say for yourself?" he asked. "Anything to say in your defense?" I shook my head no. Immediately, he was standing, his hand around my hair again, my face pulled fiercely back so that I was looking up into his gaze. The way he held my hair hurt now, and I clearly understood the message he was sending me.

"No, Sir—" I said, quickly, but not quickly enough. He had me bent over the side of the sofa in an instant, my skirt roughly pulled up to reveal the lilac rosettes adorning the tops of my garters, then yanked even higher to show my black satin panties. I heard the whisper-hiss of his belt as he pulled it free from the loops of his jeans, and then I felt the air—that crackle-shiver of moving air—before the leather connected with my upturned ass.

Fire. That was the instant vision alive in my brain. Fire. Pain
like fire, so hot and hard that I gasped for air. The pain seemed
to grow, spreading through me, flowing over me. He struck me
six times with the belt over my panties before sliding his meaty
fingers under the waistband and pulling them down. I closed
my eyes now, knowing the pain would intensify without that
filmy shield, and trying to prepare myself for this—even though
I knew that was impossible.

"Say, 'Thank you, Sir,' after every blow," he commanded.

"Thank you—" I started, but he hadn't struck me yet.

His lips were against my ear as he hissed, "Are you messing
with me, girl?"

"No, Sir!" Louder than I'd thought. Louder than I'd heard
the words in my head. I sounded like a soldier. No, Sir! Punctu-
ated fiercely with my inherent willingness to obey.

"Don't mess with me, young lady," he said, "don't test me,"
and then he kissed me, high up on my cheek, and I trembled
even more. The feeling of his gentle lips pressed to me, combined
with the knowledge that he was about to grant me a serious hiding, left me twisted and shuddering inside.

The thrashing continued, now with the belt meeting my bare
ass, and I did my best to choke out, "Thank you, Sir," after each
blow. Didn't do quite good enough, though, because he had to
continually up the intensity of the blows to keep me in line. Until
finally, he moved forward, grabbing my arms and using the belt
now to bind my wrists behind my back. Against the couch I balanced, body arched, waiting, waiting for what came next.

I'd thought about this moment all day, and it had been difficult for me to get any work done. Every time I tried to concentrate, I envisioned myself with my knickers at my ankles, ass in
the air, submitting to the punishment I so desperately craved.
Needed. Yearned for. Deserved. Every time I opened a new file,

or clicked my mouse on a spreadsheet, I lost myself in forbidden daydreams. Now, those daydreams were coming true.

I sighed, inwardly delighted, when he tested between my legs for the wetness. I felt as if only one stroke of his calloused thumb against my clit would get me off. But he didn't touch me the way I needed, changing my sighs to desperate mews.

"Not done, yet," he hissed at me. "Not quite done, yet—"

Before I fully understood what he was doing, he had me over his lap, my wrists still captured, head turned on a sofa cushion, my body in perfect position for a bare-handed spanking on my naked behind. I was already smarting, so hot from the belt, but that didn't stop him from delivering another series of stinging blows on my throbbing ass.

I squirmed my hips against his knees to gain the contact I craved, and this time, he didn't admonish me. He let me leave a wet spot on his slacks before undoing the buckle of his belt, freeing my wrists, and repositioning me over the edge of the sofa. This is the way he was going to fuck me, with my ass so hot and red from the belt and his hand, with my pussy swimming in sex juices.

He slid in and I gripped him immediately, and then he placed one hand in between the sofa and my body and began to stroke and tickle my clit as he fucked me. The sensations were almost too powerful to handle. I closed my eyes and thought about how I'd spent my day. From the second I woke up, still in bed when I planned my outfit, I'd thought of this moment. At work, when he'd called to check and see if I had been a good girl or a bad girl, I'd nearly lost it—hurrying to the bathroom to rub and rub at my clit, but unable to make myself come without the pain that he so generously dispenses.

The pain and the pleasure.

Now, as I came, I thought about our arrangement. Whenever

I wear my schoolgirl skirt out of the house, I know I'm going to get a spanking, know that I'm going to have to be taught a lesson when I get home. Know that my man will have left his expensive suit in the closet and changed into the working-class superintendent of our building, ready to dole out punishment to any needy young lady. Truth is, I can hardly get through a week without wearing something that will catch his eye and make him shake his head.

"I love it when you wear that skirt, baby—" Harry said.

I smiled as I looked down at the rumpled Burberry plaid, then imagined what I might sneak out of the house in tomorrow....

UNTOUCHED

When you start out in this world, you think you actually invented something. You're naive, right? You have the nerve to think that *you* actually invented something new. This is before you really get involved, of course, before you learn about the true underground world that exists below us. The parallel world, spinning backward on the same axis. The fringe.

Then suddenly, you get a peek behind closed doors, and you realize that there isn't anything new to invent. There isn't one single thing that someone, somewhere, hasn't already done before you. And probably a hell of a lot better than you, novice that you are.

Of course, I'm not saying that within the boundaries, things can't be changed. Without a doubt, you bring something unique to the scene, that's a fair enough statement. You'll bring your own *je ne sais quoi*, your own signature scent, but all that you own that is truly you, that is *truly* original, is your DNA. And you didn't even invent that. You've got to give your parents,

EXPOSED

your grandparents, and your ancestors credit for that.

Still, I'm hardheaded. It took me so long to learn those simple facts. It took hitting walls and trying to knock them down all by myself. Ultimately, it took meeting you to make me understand.

When I was younger, I used to try to find one place that no one else had ever stepped on—one piece of Earth to claim as my own. Walking along the beach at Pajaro Dunes in Northern California, I'd think, *No one has ever been exactly here, before.* But then I'd see a footprint, or more likely, many footprints, so I'd change the phrasing to suit my needs: *No one has ever been exactly here, wearing exactly this bathing suit; no one with black curly hair, chocolate brown eyes, and a birthmark shaped like Italy has ever stood right here right now.* (A bit too far to go to be original, huh?)

I'm laughing softly to myself, because even though I've gotten over this, I can remember that desperate feeling, the craving for being unique. For some of us have that need, to find it, to own it, to discover virginal, unclaimed land. And that's what I thought I did, the first time I let you fasten a studded collar around my throat and attach a rippling, silver chain.

New to me, that's honest enough. So new. The frighteningly sexy sensation of being harnessed for your will. Or, more honestly, for your pleasure.

But how could I have kidded myself into thinking that you and I were sexual pioneers? I'm not dumb. I knew you had to be buying our toys somewhere, that there was actually a factory churning out this stuff. Still, I managed to convince myself that the things we did, the games we played, were *ours* alone. Dressing up naughty, like your little baby-girl. Calling you Daddy, acting the role of a bad schoolgirl, your slut. Wearing skins, playing at being tough.

What a fucking joke.

When I eventually arrived on the scene, I learned that not only did I *not* invent this shit—everyone else seemed to already know about it. Everyone. It felt to me like being left out of a secret. Or not being invited to a birthday party in elementary school. I felt like a loser.

Worse than that.

I felt lost.

Ah, but I was one of the lucky few. 'Cause you found me... and claimed me...and made me your own. Untouched, I was, a journal waiting to be filled, an empty glass waiting for a shot of whiskey, a naked wrist waiting for the pull of a tight, metal cuff. Untouched, I was, and pure. And you found me and made me all dirty.

"You're mine," you said. "You are mine." First words, whispered to me in the back room of Old Joe's, whispered to me right up against my ear, because the rhythm section of the band was shaking the walls and the crowd around us was laughing loudly at some funny story the bartender had told.

I lowered my mascara-drenched lashes and inclined my head slightly toward you. I'd heard the words you said, but I wanted to be sure. You got the gesture immediately, and you slid your strong, dark arm around my waist and pulled me in closer. We couldn't have gotten any closer than that—blood and bones and thin, fine skin were the only things separating our beating hearts, and our hard/wet bodies.

"You're mine." Your arm pulled me so firmly, and I could feel the links of your silvery wallet chain digging into my thigh. "Come on, girl, time to go."

Discovered. (*No.* No. Rediscovered.)

I went, willingly (I must say that, now, willingly), followed you through the throng of multicolored, multisexed dancers, down the dark hallway, and out the back door. The cool air slapped me, stunning me, and I realized I'd left my coat under the bar stool. No worries, your strong arms were around me again, warming me, leading me to your shiny red pickup.

"Seen you around, baby, but never alone."

"We split," I said, motioning to the place on my hand where a ring used to be but now wasn't. (But it had been, understand that, there was no territory on my body that had not been previously claimed by someone else, was there?)

"Whatcha doing here, then, darling? This was his hangout, wasn't it?"

Shake of my head, of my long, black hair, letting it tickle against my cheeks and the naked part of my back that my dress didn't cover. "No, Sir. This was mine." Claim it, you get it? Make it your own.

"Okay, all right. But whatcha doin' here tonight, darling? Who you looking for?"

A step closer, a step further away from my past and toward the thrilling danger of my future—into the tight, choking hold of my present. "You." A laugh, one that didn't sound at all like my own. A laugh and an up-from-under look that was meant to be bashful, that was meant to show my faith in your power. "I was waiting for you."

No words, then, just that tight grip around my wrist, leading me to your truck. The music of your key sliding into the lock, the whisper-click of the door as it swung open, ready to swallow me up. Your hand on my ass, lifting me into the front seat. Then silence, as the world slowed down while you stalked around the front of the truck and then got in on the driver's side.

"Waiting for me," you said under your breath as the ignition caught and we exited the parking lot. "What do you know about me?"

Head lowered, staring at the crotch of my dress, wanting to

see if the wetness had spread through panties, nylons, slip, and stretchy black jersey. "I know." A beat. "I know what you can do."

Claim me. Own me. Find something new.

Your turn to laugh, now, your turn to find a joke where there was none.

"You know, huh? How do you know?"

We made a left off the main drag, into the windy streets of the bordering residential neighborhood. Not a nice neighborhood, but home to many of the patrons who hang at Old Joe's. Apartments with crumbling redbrick facades, tiny forgotten bungalows that don't take up enough space to be a threat to anyone. Yards of clotheslines connecting the buildings and colorful tatters of T-shirts and jeans pinned onto the lines, blowing in the breeze like broken and forgotten kites caught in trees.

"How'd you know?" Your voice was darker with the repetition, and I realized, quickly, that when you asked a question, you meant it to be answered.

"Trinket," I mumbled, calling the bartender, Katarina, by her nickname. "Trinket told me about you and her, about what you did together. About what *you* did to her."

"She show you, as well?"

"Yes," a pause, "Sir."

"She show you everything?"

A nod, a trembling one, and then again, "Yes, Sir."

"And you still wanted to be with me?"

No, that's not what I wanted. "No, Sir. I wanted to be... yours."

"Ah," you said, a smile in your voice, I could hear it, though I didn't dare look up. "But, darling, that's what it means. When you're with me, you are mine. That's the point, darling. That's the whole fuckin' point."

The tattoo on Trinket's back had told me as much, the drifting colors, shifting patterns. The lock in the center with the word *slave* all but carved out in bold relief. And to be yours was more than an honor—it was a lifelong commitment.

We'd reached your studio, the converted garage behind your tiny house. I'd heard of it, of course, but never been there. It's by invitation only, you understand. It's a private party, and if you don't know the password, you don't get in. I waited for you to kill the engine, waited while you climbed out of the car and walked to my side to open my door. That's the way you are. I'd heard that before. You play with etiquette the way some people twirl their hair around one finger, or bite their bottom lip with nervousness. You play with manners like a nervous twitch, holding doors open for your ladies, pulling out their chairs, paying, always paying (with cash, that is—the women you date pay with something much more dear).

Your hand slid up from my wrist to my forearm, and you closed your fist tightly, as if testing my muscles, as if wondering whether I'd have the strength to fight. I wouldn't fight, though. I wanted to tell you. Because each time you touched me it happened—I felt new. I felt molded, as your hands moved up and down my arms, squeezing, releasing, patting me.

Create me, I wanted to beg. *Make me into something new. Something yours.*

The Vasco da Gama of love...

I wondered if we'd go to the house first, or start off in the studio. I knew what I wanted, but I wasn't going to say a word until you asked me a question. The rules, again, the regulations. So important for a good scene. Deathly important for a starting relationship. Like a dance, a two-step, you have to work together. And if someone trips, if someone stumbles, there is a type of embarrassment that can destroy a budding love affair. Any good dancer will tell you that: you need to watch your partner, you need to learn from the way you are touched, from the look in your partner's eyes, from the very rhythm of his breathing.

You never watch his feet—that's not where the magic is. You watch his eyes, or you close your eyes, and you watch his soul.

And with you, there was something else, something beyond that simple, petty, one-two-three, one-two-three. There was something darker in those cavernous eyes, in the strength of your fingers, in the wisdom of your expression as you stared at me.

"So, Trinket showed you. But you still don't get it, honey, do you?"

I bit my lip to keep from saying something stupid. You were right. I didn't get it—I was functioning on a need, not on smarts at this point.

"Ask me some questions, now," you said. "I want to know what you want to know. I want to know what you're thinking."

"How many?" I mumbled, aware of how carefully you arranged the situation—you standing, me sitting, you free in the outdoors, me trapped in the metal cage of the truck. Everything with a meaning—everything with a new meaning.

"How many…women?" I said, finishing the question, knowing that you wouldn't think to guess what I had meant. That you would wait for me to be specific.

"Does it matter?"

I thought about it. "No." It didn't matter at all—I'd wondered, curiously, how many of the women at Old Joe's, at Sindy's, at Marlena's Watering Hole were yours. But it didn't affect me, either way.

"Next question." Your hand on my knee gave me the strength to continue.

"How long will it take?"

"Forever."

"To do the artwork, I mean."

"Forever."

I shook my head. "I don't understand."

"I've been waiting for you. You can understand that, can't you? I've been waiting for you as you've been waiting for me. You will be my art in progress. You will be my only one. The others—for me—were practice. That was the same way with you and him, wasn't it?"

I nodded. I hadn't even allowed myself to hope for something like this. I only wanted...what did I want? I only wanted to feel it, to feel the light that shined in Trinket's eyes. To feel the world stop beneath me, the fringe world, the parallel world, as I yawned and stretched and came, once more, to life.

"Yes, Sir," I said softly, "Yes, Sir, I understand."

"Do you want this?"

Emphatically, "Oh, yes. More than anything."

"Good." Your hand on my knee slid upward to my thigh, then my crotch, cupping me there, adding a pressure that I was not used to. "You will be mine," you said. "This is now mine."

I nodded. "Yes, Sir."

"Come with me."

I slid out of the truck bed, slammed the door, and followed you to the garage; watched you undo the padlock and chain, slide the wood door open and step outside to wait for me. I walked in ahead of you, into darkness, not able to make out anything in the room. There was a click as you flicked on the lights and the room glowed in modern beauty.

You had a tattoo parlor in your garage. The chair, the designs on the walls, the needles, the ink. You had everything, sterile, perfectly in place. Beaming skulls grinned down at me. Roses curled with daggers. Tigers pranced back and forth.

Skeletons shimmered in stark black line. All done by your hand. All done by a master.

"You don't get to choose," you said, talking casually as you began to set up the needles and inks.

"I know."

"But you can let me know what you like."

I wandered around, looking at the walls, trying to decide which scrolling piece I liked the best. Because they'd all been created by you, I could not choose one over the other. Each had a stark beauty, an inner glow, unlike any of the work I'd seen by artists in other tattoo parlors.

"You don't like anything?"

"I like everything."

Now you put down your instruments and came over to me, catching my face between your hands and kissing me. "You know that I do this for a living, right?"

"Yes."

"You know that in the future I will tattoo other people?"

"Yes."

"But from now on I tattoo you only with my own designs. You don't choose from the walls. You don't pick tigers and ladies behind partially opened doors. No ravens in windows. No pinup Bettys. I create art for your body, for your skin, and you close your eyes and feel the pain of the needle as it reaches beneath your skin, as it reaches to your soul."

"Yes."

"You will be mine." You looked at me with your dark eyes in your dark face. "No, no, you're already mine."

You led me to the chair and after a moment's thought, fastened me down with leather straps. Then, slowly, you slid a pair of steel scissors underneath the hem of my dress and cut all the way to the neckline. The cold metal against my skin made me tremble, but I remained as still as I could as you parted the two halves of the dress and revealed my pale skin.

Your fingers tested each part of my exposed body, the way an artist checks a canvas to make sure it is evenly stretched over a frame. You stroked my throat, my breasts, the sides of my ribs. You placed the palms of both hands against my belly, feeling the spot where my pulse still raced. You cupped your hand again over my mound of pubis (through my panties) and smiled as you felt the wetness seep through the crotch and to your fingers.

"We'll start tonight," you said. "I will not tell you what I am drawing. I will not be working from a set design, only from the pictures I see in my mind."

"Yesss…"

Claim me. Own me. Find something new.

Quickly, you prepared the needle, choosing the first color, dark blood red, and moving in close. And, with your assistance, I did invent something new. With your help, I reinvented *myself*.

DON'T LOOK
BACK

Google him. Sometimes occasionally, if I've got a minute to kill while the printer is churning out my latest project. Sometimes obsessively, staring at the computer screen until my eyes water, drinking straight vodka as the minutes blur. Sometimes reck-lessly—not bothering to delete my history afterward. "Deleting history" seems like too much of a cheat. It would be danger-ously easy to strike out all the pages I've visited on my endless, circular search. You can't do that in real life.

I know he isn't the doctor in Minneapolis who specializes in exotic-sounding diseases, or the professor on sabbatical in the Orient who beams his latest pictures up to his website every two or three days—lovely lush landscapes that I've grown fond of viewing. Sure, people change, but not *that* much. I'm absolutely certain he's not one of a pair of Bluegrass-loving brothers who live in Utah. They hit local bars every few weeks, playing warm-up for bands I've never heard of.

I've done the online White Pages searches, as well, turning up addresses from fifteen years ago, six or seven places in a row, apartments I remember visiting when I cut class to fuck him. I actually think about calling the numbers—one might be current—but I can't make myself. There was no caller ID back then. Now, I might get caught. And what would happen to my well-ordered life if he star-69ed me and my sweet boyfriend answered?

So I resort to Googling.

Googling takes the place of those late-night drive-bys, looking to see if his Harley was in the spot out front of his building. My muscles tighten up the same way now as they did back then. Maybe I'll see him. Maybe I won't. So why do I even bother? Because I fantasize that one day when I type in his name, up will come all the information that I crave. What he's been doing for the past decade and a half. What he's doing now. Who he's with. How he's aged.

Truthfully, I don't know all that much about him. If I were to tally up all the facts, they wouldn't fill an index card. Or a matchbook cover. He was older than me, but by exactly how much, I don't know. Twenty-seven to my eighteen. That's what I remember, but he lied all the time. He could have been lying about that. In my online search, I found a man with his name who graduated high school in 1978 somewhere in Southern California. Is that him? His middle initial was *D*, but he never told me what it stood for. Donald? David? Daniel? Dean? None of those seem right, yet I've found men with those middle names on the Internet. Might he be one of them?

There's a fellow in the Midwest who runs marathons. I can't imagine Mark breaking a sweat unless he were running from a cop. But he had a sleek runner's physique way back when. Could he have transformed himself into an athlete? Has he given up pot in favor of healthier substances? Has he hit the pavement to kill his demons?

Googling takes my mind off my modern-day problems. Googling makes me forget about deadlines and pressures and what we're going to have for dinner. Delivery pizza, again? Sounds good. Far easier to answer that mundane query than the other nagging questions pulling on me until my stomach aches: Should I pay the $29.95 and do a search of prison records? Because that's where I'll find him. I'm sure of it.

I don't enter my credit card. I don't think I actually want to know.

After spending hours on the computer, I dream about him. My eyes hurt and my head spins. I hit the pillow and recreate his image from the puzzle pieces that I remember: The black-ink tattoo on his upper arm. The way his blue eyes could turn gray or green depending on what he was wearing. Depending, even, on his mood. His paint-splattered jeans. His gray shirt. His body.

Oh, god, his body.

I remember our first date, if you can call it a date. A walk from the beauty supply store where I worked after school back to my home—with a lengthy sojourn in a deserted alley behind the beauty supply. And I remember our first kiss—moments into our first date. What was I doing out in the rapidly darkening twilight with him? Who was looking out for me? He was.

He pushed me up against a wall and kissed me so ferociously that there are days I swear I can still feel his lips on mine. When I run my tongue over my bottom lip I feel where he bit me. Can you feel a kiss fifteen years later? You bet you can.

His large, warm hands gripped my wrists over my head while his powerful body held mine in place. He pressed against me, and I could tell how hard he was, and I could understand—finally—what all those whispers about sex were about. I hadn't gotten it before. Look, I wasn't an idiot. Just naive. I knew where babies came from. I'd watched enough old movies to understand the steaminess of the looks between hero and heroine. But there'd been no appeal to me in the high school fumblings at dances. In the background make-out sessions at parties. I'd been an outsider, an alien, gazing wistfully from a distance and knowing for certain that nothing present was right for me.

With Mark, everything was different.

In that back alley behind the cosmetic store where I was a shopgirl, he slid a hand up under my shirt and ran his fingers over my pale pink satin bra. In a flash, I wished that the bra was made of black lace instead. He touched my breasts firmly, as if he owned them, as if he owned me. He took my clothes off, unbuttoning my jeans himself, pulling my shirt up over my head, exposing me for what I really was.

"A slut," he said. "You're my little slut—"

I shivered, but stayed silent. I knew who the sluts were at school. I knew that I wasn't one.

"Aren't you? Tell the truth." His hands were everywhere. His mouth on my neck, his fingers pulling down my panties and parting my lips to see how wet I was.

"Come on, Carla. Tell the truth—"

I Google him. Endlessly. Dangerously. Desperately.

Because he knew me. I was just out, taking that first shy step out into the world...and he knew me.

I understand why I do it. So why the hell do I find it so odd that he Googles me, too? That I get an email, short but not sweet, asking if I'm the one he remembers.

Yeah, I am. Sure I am. Of course I am.

I think I am.

Mark waits for me in our spot, leaning against a gray concrete wall, looking almost exactly the same despite a fifteen-year absence. Do I look the same, too? I'm not. Not a teenager anymore, not trembling with desire, not—dare I say it?—young.

But I was young. Back then, I was new.

We were inseparable for months; me, a high school kid, and this twenty-seven-year-old hoodlum. This handsome, so handsome man with the cold blue eyes out of a Who song and the iron jawline. A man who seemed to know everything about me. What was I doing? What was I thinking? Christ, what am I thinking now, fifteen years later? He's in his forties, but still effortlessly lean and tough with only the slightest lines around his eyes and the same tall, hard body I remember. I have on jeans and a black sleeveless T-shirt that says, *I break things* on the front, something I dug out of a box filled with memories in the attic. I can pass for twenty-three rather than thirty-three if I have to. My dark hair is long to my shoulders, my glossy bangs in my eyes, as always.

He doesn't say a word. He just looks at me. I close my eyes tight and remember—the loss of him when he disappeared, the way no boy could replace him after he was gone. I spent years trying to recreate the exact connection that we'd had. I slutted myself out with a variety of losers, all of whom possessed at least one rebellious quality of Mark's, none of whom owned the whole package. Some spanked me. Some fucked me in public places. None made me feel anything other than disillusioned. Ultimately, I gave up hope. Now, even though I am with someone else, I've come running at Mark's call.

What the *fuck* am I doing here?

"Carla," he says, hands in my thick hair, lips on mine, and it is suddenly summertime again, and I'm missing him.

"Carla," he says, and I open my eyes and I look at him, and

see him, the man, the danger, the reason I'm who I am today. If I hadn't met him in high school, who would I have become? Some other girl. Some smart chick. Not a person who would leave a loving relationship in order to track down that fleeting emotion of lust from a decade and a half ago. Not a moron who could still go weak-kneed at the first sight of her longtime crush.

"What do you need, baby?" he asks, and I find myself cradled in his strong arms, as always, my legs shaky, my heart pounding at triple speed so that I can feel the timpani-throb in my chest and hear the clatter in my ears. "Can you say it, now? Can you tell Daddy what you need?"

My throat grows tight. There's a man at home, waiting for me. A simple man with a true soul who does not know where I am, but who trusts me to always return nonetheless. Yet suddenly the very concept of trust seems immensely overrated. What's trust to lust? Which emotion would win every time?

"Carla," Mark says. Just that word. Just my name, and I am lost all over again, head spinning, heart dying.

"Let's go."

He has no power over me. I'm not a kid anymore. You can't impress me with a stolen Harley. You can't turn me into a puddle with a single kiss. I'm only here on a crazy dare. I'm only here because of Google. I can leave him. I can run. I have a safe home furnished with faux antiques from Pottery Barn and appliances purchased only after careful consideration of the advice of *Consumers' Choice*. I have a place to be. Mark doesn't own me, not any part of me.

"Come on, baby."

I suppose I've hidden it well, the desires that burn in me. I chose normal over interesting. I chose safety over adventure.

"You know you want to."

Back then, I'd never have been so fucking lame. Back then,

I'd always take the risks when offered. Jesus, I invented the risks when there were none available. Slipping out my bedroom window to meet him. Cutting class to ride to his apartment on the back of his pilfered Harley. Letting him handcuff me to his bed frame so that he could do anything he wanted to me. Anything at all.

Can I change? Is it too late?

My hand is trapped in his, held so tightly. The heat between us is palpable. Some people never find that heat. That summertime heat that melts over your body and leaves you breathless. Some people search their whole miserable fucking lives for some semblance of a sizzling kiss, and they die believing that "true love always" is just a bitter myth. But I found that heat as a teenage kid and I knew for real that it existed. Even if I'd never found it again, I'd had it once.

How many places have I looked? How many other dark alleys have I gone down with nameless, faceless men, trying to find that old summertime magic from years ago?

Mark bends to kiss my neck and I remember in a flash, in one of those blinding jolts, that he'd covered me in suntan oil one sultry afternoon. I'd spent the whole day at the beach, the first truly hot spring day, and he'd come to my house afterward and dumped out the contents of my red-striped canvas tote bag on my floor and found that bottle of oil. My group of friends had no fear of wrinkles yet, no worry about sun damage, not like the ladies in my circle now, the ones who Google StriVectin with the same passion as mine for Googling this man. We used the oil back then, for "the San Tropez tan." Mark coated his strong hands while he told me to strip, and I watched his hands for a moment, dripping with the oil, knowing what he was going to do.

I remember being shy, so nervous, still unaccustomed to being naked in front of a man. I could strip at the gym, in front of

my peers, but taking off my clothes while he watched was something entirely different. Mark liked me like that. Not just naked,
but nervous. He liked to put me off center, to make me feel as if
I were always on a teeter-totter, the ground rushing up to meet
me when I fell. He watched through half-shut eyes that told me
of his appreciation as I slowly took off my pink halter top, my
cutoff jeans, my candy-colored bikini top and bottoms.

And then he covered me with the scented liquid until I
gleamed, shiny and gold, the smell of papaya and coconut swirling around us. He rubbed the oil into my breasts, and over my
flat belly, and down my hips. He coated me with the shimmering
liquid, and then he fucked me like that, slippery and glistening,
staining my sheets, ruining his pants.

Nobody had fucked me like that before.

Nobody's fucked me like that since.

"Come on, Carla," he says now, leading me from the non-
descript alley to the parking lot in back. There is a pickup truck
waiting. I know it's his. He always drove motorcycles or pick-
ups. They suited him. I look behind us, take one last look like
Lot's doomed wife. I could go back, wander through the alley,
hit the shelves in the nearby Borders, buy the latest issue of *Al-
lure* magazine, get an iced coffee in the cafe. I could go back to
beige and safety and predictability. To reviews in *Consumers'*.
To my Mr. Coffee machine—a six-time winner.

"What do you need, Carla? Tell Daddy what you need."

Back in high school, I'd needed to be spanked, and he'd
taken care of that need with the most exquisite care. He hadn't
laughed at me. He hadn't refused my desires or been disgusted
by them. He'd simply assumed the role, once I confessed. Once
I'd finally gotten the nerve and spelled it out.

I'd needed him to bend me over his lap and lower my jeans.

I'd needed his firm hand on my naked ass, punishing me. Or his belt, whispering seductively in the air before it connected with my pale skin. Then I'd needed him to cuff me to his bed and fuck me, to flip me over and fuck my ass until I cried. Until I screamed. Is that what he'd seen on the day we met? A yearning in my eyes that told him I was in need? How had he found me? How had he known?

Most importantly, I'd needed him to show me that I wasn't a freak for having the cravings that I did, the white-hot yearnings that kept me up late at night, kept me away from the high school boys and the safety of what I was supposed to do and who I was supposed to be, and he'd given me everything I needed.

Don Henley says: *You can never look back.*

"What do you need, now?" Mark murmurs, lips to my ear. I know suddenly what I don't need. I don't need to erase my history with a keystroke, when history is all that I've got.

My fingertips grip the door handle of his vintage blue Ford. I swing the door open and climb inside.

You know, I never liked Don Henley much anyway.

ABOUT THE AUTHOR

Called "a trollop with a laptop" by the *East Bay Express*, Alison Tyler is naughty and she knows it. Over the past decade, Ms. Tyler has written more than twenty explicit novels, including *Learning to Love It*, *Strictly Confidential*, *Sweet Thing*, *Sticky Fingers*, and *Something About Workmen* (all published by Black Lace), as well as *Rumors*, *Tiffany Twisted*, and the upcoming *With or Without You* (all published by Cheek). Her novels and short stories have been translated into Japanese, Dutch, German, Italian, Norwegian, and Spanish. Her stories have appeared in anthologies including *Stirring Up a Storm* (Thunder's Mouth Press), *Hot Women's Erotica* (Blue Moon Books), *Sex Toy Tales* (Down There Press), *Noirotica 3* (Black Books), *Best S/M Erotica* (Black Books), *Mammoth Book of Best New Erotica* (Carrol & Graf), and *Up All Night* (Alyson); and in *Sweet Life* and *Sweet Life 2*, *Taboo*, *Best Women's Erotica* (2002, 2003, 2005, and 2006), *Best of Best Women's Erotica*, *Erotic Travels Tales* and *Erotic Travels Tales 2*, *Best Fetish Erotica*, *Lips Like*

Sugar, and *Best Lesbian Erotica 1996* (all published by Cleis); and in *Wicked Words* (4, 5, 6, 8, and 10), *Sex in the Office*, *Sex on Holiday*, *Best of Black Lace 2*, and *Sex in Uniform* (all published by Black Lace); as well as in *Playgirl* magazine, *Penthouse Variations*, and *His&Hers* magazine. Her ultra-short stories are featured in *The Ultimate Guide to Fellatio*, *The Ultimate Guide to Cunnilingus*, and *The Ultimate Guide to Sexual Fantasy*, all edited by Violet Blue and published by Cleis.

She is the editor of *Batteries Not Included* (Diva); *Heat Wave*, *Best Bondage Erotica* and *Best Bondage Erotica 2*, *The Merry XXXmas Book of Erotica*, *Luscious*, *Red Hot Erotica*, *Slave to Love,* and *Three-Way* (all from Cleis Press); *Naughty Fairy Tales from A to Z* (Plume); and the *Naughty Stories from A to Z* series, the *Down & Dirty* series, *Naked Erotica*, and *Juicy Erotica* (all from Pretty Things Press). Please visit www.prettythingspress.com.

Ms. Tyler is loyal to coffee (black), lipstick (red), and tequila (straight). She has tattoos, but no piercings; a wicked tongue, but a quick smile; and bittersweet memories, but no regrets. She believes it won't rain if she doesn't bring an umbrella, prefers hot and dry to cold and wet, and loves to spout her favorite motto: "You can sleep when you're dead." She chooses Led Zeppelin over the Beatles, the Cure over NIN, and the Stones over everyone—yet although she appreciates good rock, she has a pitiful weakness for eighties hair bands.

In all things important, she remains faithful to her partner of ten years, but she still can't choose just one perfume.

> *Expose yourself to your deepest fear; after that,*
> *fear has no power, and the fear of freedom shrinks*
> *and vanishes. You are free.*
>
> —JIM MORRISON